REBEL
POWER PLAY

DAVID SKUY

Scholastic Canada Ltd.

Toronto New York London Auckland Sydney
Mexico City New Delhi Hong Kong Buenos Aires

Scholastic Canada Ltd.
604 King Street West, Toronto, Ontario M5V 1E1, Canada
Scholastic Inc.
557 Broadway, New York, NY 10012, USA
Scholastic Australia Pty Limited
PO Box 579, Gosford, NSW 2250, Australia
Scholastic New Zealand Limited
Private Bag 94407, Botany, Manukau 2163, New Zealand
Scholastic Children's Books
Euston House, 24 Eversholt Street, London NW1 1DB, UK

www.scholastic.ca

Library and Archives Canada Cataloguing in Publication
Skuy, David, 1963-
        Rebel power play / David Skuy.
(Game time)
ISBN 978-0-545-98625-0
        I. Title. II. Series: Game time.
PS8637.K88 R42 2009   jC813'.6   C2009-901291-X

ISBN-10 0-545-98625-7

Front cover image © Zoran Milich/Masterfile
Back cover image © iStockphoto.com/AndrewJohnson

    6 5 4 3 2   Printed in Canada 139   14 15 16 17

TABLE OF CONTENTS

To Kelly — who loved to play,
although for too short a time.

1

CLOSE CALL

Charlie readied himself for the shot.

"Eat some yellow tennis ball," the shooter said, and he launched a blistering slapshot.

Partly screened by two players, Charlie threw out his arm in desperation. The ball nicked the blocker and deflected up over his shoulder.

Clunk!

It hit the crossbar and bounced back in front of the net. Four players scrambled madly for it. Charlie dropped into a butterfly to protect the lower half of the net. The shooter got control of the ball and cut hard to the far post. Out of position, Charlie sprawled on his back and held up his catcher.

Whack.

The shooter banged his stick on the pavement. He'd fired it right into Charlie's glove. Charlie laughed as he got to his feet. Talk about lucky saves!

"Admit it — that was highway robbery," the shooter demanded.

"Not my fault you can't score on an open net, Scott," Charlie replied.

He took off his goalie mask. He was tired — they'd

been playing for two hours — but he wasn't about to stop. It was tough enough to even get his friends to play road hockey. The hockey season had started a week ago, and now they were all too busy to hang out. That was life, he supposed. It wouldn't be so bad if he played for a team too, but he hadn't arrived in Terrence Falls until the beginning of the school year, so he'd missed the spring tryouts.

"I'll give you dudes one more chance to score on me," he said.

Charlie curled his stick around the ball and flicked it down the driveway. The ball bounced between Scott's legs and rolled down the driveway all the way to the other side of the street.

Scott rolled his eyes. "Great, Joyce. Now someone has to get it back."

"I'm just trying to get you in shape for the hockey season," Charlie said. "So be a good boy and fetch."

Instead, Scott walked over to the front lawn and flopped to the grass. "I'm starving. Any of you hiding a burger and fries in his pocket?" he said. "Pudge, did you bring any goodies from your dad's restaurant?"

"Sorry, Scott. I thought you might last a few minutes without eating."

"A few minutes — are you insane?"

"Does your new coach know about your weight problem?" Nick asked.

"What weight problem?"

"You'll see," Nick said.

Scott threw a clump of dirt in reply, which Nick avoided by dropping to the ground.

"I have an old sandwich in my knapsack," Nick said.

"It's from two days ago and I might've dropped it on the ground a few times, but . . ."

"I can't believe you've been holding out on me," Scott said. "I thought we were friends. Fork it over."

"Make me."

"We'll settle it like men — thumb wrestle! Two out of three."

"I got my money on Nick," Zachary called out.

"Ten bucks on Scott," Pudge said.

They obviously didn't want to play street hockey anymore. But Charlie wasn't in the mood to joke around.

"I'll see what we've got in the kitchen," Charlie said quietly.

When he went inside, he found his mom washing the floor.

"Stop right there, young man," she said. "I don't want you dragging your dirty shoes all over."

"Sorry, Mom. Just wondered if there was something to munch. Some of the guys — well, Scott, actually — are kind of hungry."

His mom laughed. "I swear that boy eats enough to feed ten people."

"He won the school hot dog eating contest — ten in only five minutes, including the bun. A new record."

"Very impressive. Give me a few minutes for the floor to dry and I'll dig something up."

"Thanks, Mom . . . and we don't need anything special. Chips or something would be cool."

"Charlie, I have a reputation to uphold. It wouldn't look good for a café owner to serve junk food."

"Don't worry about it — keep it simple."

"Leave it to me."

He knew there was no point arguing, so he left. He was proud of his mom. She'd only opened her café a month ago, and it was already doing great. She was a really good cook. Still, it was embarrassing when friends came over and she baked cookies or a cake, as if he was still a little kid.

When he went outside, Scott and Nick were balancing on their heads. Zachary and Pudge were cheering them on. "What're they up to now?" Charlie said.

"Thumb war didn't settle it," Pudge said. "They've moved on to a headstand competition."

"Hey, Zachary, how was practice today?" Charlie asked.

"Kinda cool. A power skating coach who once tried out for the Chicago Blackhawks had us doing all sorts of intense drills. Major tempo. I was totally wiped out by the end."

"How's the team look?"

Zachary shrugged. "We have a solid crew. The Snow Birds won the championship last year, and I guess we're favoured to win again. The Wildcats are supposed to be good too."

He couldn't help feeling a bit jealous. Zachary made it sound as if playing for the Snow Birds was no big deal. But that was Zachary — he was laid back about everything.

"What about you, Pudge? You changed your mind about the Wildcats?" he asked.

"Are you kidding? No way I'd play with Jake — not to mention Liam and Thomas. And Coach Schultz is too over the top. He was always on my case, ranting about something or other. I was on that team for two years — two years too many, as far as I'm concerned."

He understood about not wanting to play with Jake and his friends. They'd bullied Pudge for years, and had made Charlie's life miserable from the first day of school. He was one happy camper when they transferred from his homeroom. He did owe them one thing, though. He had become friends with Pudge because of their bullying. They had stood up to them together. Charlie thought of Pudge as his best friend, though he doubted Pudge thought the same — they'd only met a month ago. Pudge wasn't funny like Scott, or a terrific athlete like Nick, or cool like Zachary. He was just someone you could trust. At least he and Pudge could hang together a bit since neither of them had a team.

"I've called around to all the triple-A and double-A teams — I couldn't even get a tryout," Charlie said. "Have you heard of anything lately?"

Pudge reddened slightly. "Forgot to tell you. The Tornadoes invited me out. My dad knows the coach . . . from the restaurant . . . and . . . well . . . I signed with them." He cleared his throat and looked down at the ground before continuing. "I asked if they had a spot for you." He shrugged. "Coach said they were full up."

"Great. I'm the only guy without a team."

Charlie instantly regretted his words. He sounded angry, and Pudge was clearly embarrassed. But Pudge hadn't done anything wrong. He had a right to play.

Scott ran over with his arms over his head.

"All hail the headstand champion of the world. Bow before me, mortals."

Nick was right behind. "He lies."

Scott flashed a grin. "Maybe I didn't exactly win. But Nick cheats and everyone knows it." He put his arm around Charlie's shoulders. "So where's that grub?"

"It's coming. My mom's on it."

"Awesome. I hope she brings those chocolate chip cookies," Scott said.

"I'm hoping for the raspberry tarts," Nick said.

"The ones with the whipped cream around the edges?" Scott said. "Those babies rock."

"Tell me about your team," Charlie said, "to take your mind off your stomach."

Scott stretched out on the grass, and put his hands behind his head. "The Hornets will be the team to beat, no doubt. We've got two good goalies. And, with me on defence, the blue line is solid — naturally. And we got a couple of guys up front with skills."

"You told me you've got practically the same lineup as last year," Nick said.

"We do."

"The Hornets finished three points out of last place."

"New season — new attitude."

"Same players — same results."

Pudge interrupted. "I bet Charlie would be able to help you guys."

Scott's tone grew serious. "I asked the coach. He told me the league only allows him to sign seventeen players, and he'd already committed back in April. He did say that if someone drops out he'd love to have you. Tough spot to be in, Joyce. I mean, after how well you played in the Champions Cup last month for our school team, I figured you'd be a lock for a triple-A spot."

"I'm not sweating it too much," Charlie said bravely. "I bet something will come up. I may not play competitive hockey this season, but that's cool. I'll just be ready for the spring tryouts for next season."

It killed him to think that — but he wasn't going to be a whiner.

"I'm here for you if you need a good cry," Scott said.

That earned him a clump of dirt from each of the guys.

Charlie stood to take off his pads. His father had given them to him two years ago. The insides were all worn, and the lining at the bottom was coming apart. They were also too short. Scott had blasted a shot off his ankle, and he could feel the bruise coming up. He'd never think of getting new ones, though. He'd rather suffer a thousand bruises. He didn't have many things left to remind him of his father.

He fought a wave of bitterness. It was still hard to think about his father dying in that car accident.

"No better feeling than taking off goalie pads," Charlie said, holding one up.

Scott grinned. "It's a good look for you. Gives you that ultra-dope waddle when you walk."

"Show me." Charlie tossed the pad at him.

"Chawie! Chawie! Josh have ball. Josh fwo ball."

Charlie looked up and felt his heart rise to his throat. His three-year-old neighbour from across the street was standing in the middle of the road, holding a ball and giggling — totally oblivious to the car racing towards him!

"Josh, car!" Charlie screamed.

Josh froze and dropped the ball. Charlie felt things happen in slow motion, as if he were watching himself in a movie. With one goalie pad still on, he ran towards Josh, scooped him up in his left arm and catapulted himself towards the curb. They tumbled to the road. Josh began to shriek, thrashing and kicking.

"You're okay," Charlie said. "It's over." A wave of relief washed over him.

"Joshie! Joshie! Are you all right? Are you hurt?"

"I think he's good, Mr. Hume," Charlie said.

Josh ran to his father and jumped into his arms.

Charlie hadn't known his neighbours long, but he'd noticed how Mr. Hume doted on his son. They were always together. It had been like that with his own dad.

Josh stopped crying.

By this time Charlie's friends had surrounded them.

"You guys good?" Pudge asked.

Charlie nodded.

"That was fun," Josh said, which made everyone laugh.

"Hume! What kind of parent are you?"

It was the driver. Charlie got to his feet and slid over to join his friends. He found the guy kind of intimidating. He was tall and well built, and his eyes had dark circles underneath that gave him a menacing appearance. His clothes looked expensive. Charlie couldn't stop looking at his enormous gold watch. It covered almost his entire wrist. He'd never seen a watch like that.

He looked over at Mr. Hume, whose face had flushed deeply. Mr. Hume lowered his eyes and shrugged.

"I was washing the car,' he said weakly. "Guess I took my eyes off Josh for a second, Mr. Dunn."

"Pay attention," he replied. "Little kid like that — you can't let them out of your sight. Lucky I hit the brakes in time. Not many drivers have my reaction time."

"I'm grateful," Mr. Hume said.

Charlie didn't buy that. Dunn was speeding — and he hadn't hit the brakes fast enough. In fact, Charlie was pretty sure he'd been talking on a cell phone.

Dunn crouched down in front of Josh. "You watch yourself, little buddy. Promise me there'll be no more running onto the street."

Josh hid behind his dad's legs.

Dunn grunted and stood up. "That reminds me," he said. "Hume, get to the store early tomorrow, around seven. We have a new shipment of hockey gear to organize."

"I'll be there, Mr. Dunn." He cleared his throat. "See you then. I think I'll take Josh inside." He picked up Josh and turned to go. "Thanks," he whispered as he passed Charlie.

"Bye, Chawie," Josh said over his dad's shoulder.

The boys gathered together. Dunn put his hands on his hips. Charlie wished he'd leave. He made things weird.

"Don't some of you attend Terrence Falls High School?"

No one answered for a few moments.

"We all do," Charlie said finally.

Dunn swung around and looked right at Charlie.

"My son goes there — Mike Dunn. You know him?"

Charlie nodded. "We're all in grade nine with Mike."

"Any of you hockey players?"

This time they all nodded.

"Are you any good?"

Charlie exchanged looks with his friends. How were they supposed to answer that? Fortunately, they didn't have to. Dunn continued without waiting for a reply.

"You're all minor bantam age, so this may be of interest — that's if you can really play. The triple-A division of the East Metro Hockey League is about to change forever. The Aeros lost their sponsor about a week ago and had to pack it in. They've never done much anyway. I don't think the league was too heartbroken that they folded. Anyway, the league went looking for a replacement team — and yours truly answered the call."

Charlie had spoken to the Aeros' coach. At least this explained why he'd been so vague about a tryout.

Dunn continued. "I've always thought about taking over a team — grabbing the helm and building a winner — a powerhouse. So that's just what I'm gonna do. And believe me, when I decide to do something — I do it. Nothing stands in my way. That's what got me where I am today."

Charlie had never heard anyone speak with such confidence.

"How many players are you looking for?" Charlie asked.

"I've already signed a few. But I need at least ten more solid players — guys with real potential and the right attitude. If you guys think you fit the bill, give it a shot. Tryouts start in two days. Team's called the Hawks. Take my card and give me a call if you're interested."

He gave a bunch of cards to Charlie, flipped his keys in his hand, winked and went back to his car. The engine roared and he set off at high speed, the tires screeching as he pulled away. No one said a word until he was out of sight.

He looked at the card: *Tom Dunn, President, Dunn's Sportsmart.*

"Charlie, I have one question," Scott said. "When did you have time to find a phone booth and change into your Superman costume before saving that kid?"

He didn't answer.

"Joyce?" Scott prompted.

"Umm . . . I don't know." He was too excited by the news to listen. It was perfect — a AAA team in Terrence Falls with ten open spots. That meant he had a shot at playing competitive hockey this season — or, better yet, they could all play for the Hawks! That would be way cool. Hockey was practically the most important thing in his life. It was the only thing that had made things bearable after his father died and they moved to Terrence Falls. And now, out of nowhere, some guy decides to sponsor a brand-new team. It was like a miracle.

"Can you believe it?" Charlie said. "Isn't it too bizarre for words?"

"Is what too bizarre for words?" Pudge asked.

They were all staring at him. Didn't they get it?

"The Hawks . . . the new team. We could all play together. It would be like the school team — only bet-

ter, because instead of just playing a weekend tournament, we'd be on the same team for a whole season. We
almost won the Champions Cup — we could even give
the Snow Birds a serious battle."

No one said a word. He wondered what they were
thinking.

"I never thought of it that way," Pudge said. "It's
an interesting idea, I guess."

"It's more than interesting," he responded. "It's,
like, totally interesting. It's, like, over-the-top interesting. What could be—"

Nick interrupted. "What about the commitments
we signed? It seems a bit bogus to quit two weeks
before the start of the regular season."

They walked back to the lawn. What could he say to
that? He searched his brain for an answer.

"Nick, I see your point. On the other hand, this is a
once-in-a-lifetime opportunity. Sure, we can all play on
separate teams, play it safe this year. But I say, take a
chance and play together. Think about the school team.
Pudge and Zachary, we could be on the same line again.
Scott and Nick, you could be defence partners again."

"My dad would kill me after he made all those calls
to the other coaches," Pudge said.

Scott and Nick seemed deep in thought. Charlie
turned to Zachary.

"I know giving up a spot on the Snow Birds is
tough. They've got an awesome lineup. But that team is
stacked. You'd just be another player. On the Hawks
you'd be a star and get twice the ice time. It'd be cool
to have you on my wing. I bet we'd lead the league in
goals."

Zachary nodded, but didn't say anything. He looked away.

This was going nowhere. Maybe Pudge . . .

"How about my left winger?"

Pudge returned his gaze for a moment. Charlie grew hopeful. There was something about the look in his eye.

"It is an interesting idea, I guess," Pudge said.

Not exactly an over-the-top reaction — better than a no, at least.

"Maybe you guys can think about it. I'm gonna take a shot and, well . . . it'll be cool either way. We can play on the same team or against each other. I wouldn't mind dangling Scott with the puck a few times."

"Science fiction, Joyce," Scott said. "I'm too inside your head to fall for your bogus moves. But wait till you play Nick. He tends to wet himself and get distracted."

Nick pretended to be horrified. "I thought you weren't gonna tell the boys about that . . . problem."

"No secrets among friends — although I kinda put that on Facebook," Scott said.

Nick shrugged. "As long as it's only all the kids at school."

They started cracking jokes about how their teams stacked up against each other. Charlie couldn't really join in. The Hawks weren't even a team yet. The conversation gave him a chance to think about it, however. The Hawks gave him a real chance to play in the top league after all, and maybe Pudge would switch since he didn't know guys on his team. Matt was also looking for a team. He used to play for the Wildcats, and since the school tournament he'd become a friend. Matt didn't like Jake any more than Charlie or Pudge did. He had to accept that Scott, Nick and Zachary probably wouldn't leave established teams — especially Zachary. The Snow Birds were a dynasty.

"Anyone hungry?" his mom called out.

Scott leapt to his feet.

"There's enough for everyone," his mom laughed.

"Not if I eat it all first," Scott replied, racing up the steps into the house.

"I'll give you a call later to talk about the Hawks," Charlie said to Pudge as they followed.

Pudge nodded, but didn't say anything.

Charlie could have punched himself. The guy was obviously not into it. It was stupid to expect anyone to quit a team just to play with him. Plain dumb. He needed to be cool about it. It would be enough just to make the Hawks.

Charlie forced himself to grin, and he laughed along with the others as Scott struggled to stuff two bananas into his mouth on a dare from Nick.

HAWK TALK

Charlie locked his bike to the fence and headed to the front doors of the school. The bell hadn't gone yet! His homeroom teacher, Mr. Hilton, had given him a serious lecture yesterday about being on time, and he didn't want to get on his bad side.

He looked around for a familiar face. Things were a bit better at school lately, at least compared to a month ago when he didn't know anyone. Lunch period had been torture then. Now he could hang with some of the guys from the tournament team. A loud voice caught his attention. Jake was talking to Liam and Thomas. His three least favourite people.

There was also a new kid with them. He was huge, even bigger than Jake. There were a couple of girls too — including Julia Chow! That bugged him. Why would she be hanging out with Jake and his lame crew?

"Whatever," he muttered, and walked off to the side. He leaned against the wall. No big deal. He'd learned to be by himself since coming to this school. Then he spotted Pudge near the parking lot. He was talking to Mike Dunn, and another kid Charlie didn't know. Mike didn't have much time for Charlie — and frankly, the feeling was mutual. Mike was a show-off, always bragging. But since his father was sponsoring the Hawks, it made sense to be friendly.

"What's up?" Charlie asked.

Pudge pointed at Mike. "He's filling me in on the Hawks."

"Rumour has it you're thinking of trying out," Mike said.

"I'm pretty stoked. All the other teams are full — and I spoke to every coach about ten times. My season was about to go down the drain — until I heard about the Hawks."

"You're kinda counting your chickens a bit early, aren't you?" Mike said.

"What do you mean?"

"Tryouts start tomorrow. No one's made the team yet — except for a few key players." He laughed and slapped his friend's back. He stared at Charlie defiantly.

His dad was the sponsor, so naturally Mike would be on the team. Charlie knew that. Still, he could tone it down. The guy was hard to take. He decided to ignore the diss. No point getting into it now.

"Fair enough. I only meant I'm going to give it a shot, and if I make it, then cool."

Mike shrugged. "I should tell you that centre is taken, so don't get your hopes up about playing there."

"You've got three centres who can outplay Charlie?" Pudge asked.

"Don't worry about it," Charlie said. "We'll see what happens at the tryouts. I don't care where I play."

"Team's going to be awesome," Mike said. "And centre is spoken for — so deal."

"Centre's not an issue. I just want to play—"

Mike cut him off. "You should count yourself lucky if you make the team. We're going to build a power-house — keep the team together for a few years and rack up some trophies. The right players gotta be there from the start. There's a major tournament in Boston we're going to, and we may even train in Sweden next year."

"That's going to cost a lot," Charlie said.

Mike laughed. "Don't worry about money. You win by doing things right — that means first class, dude. The sponsor's going to make sure of that." He winked at his friend. "If any other guys from school are think-ing of trying out, tell them there are no guarantees. Coach is looking for character — real hockey players. No room on the team for scared little boys."

Charlie fought to control his temper. Mike was way out of line, since he was only on the team because of his dad.

"What about goalie?" Pudge said. "I bet the best goalies have already committed."

"Taken care of, dude." Mike shook hands with his friend, adding a back slap for good measure. The boy grinned and puffed out his chest. "This is our goalie — Simon Godfrey."

Simon thrust his chin upwards. Charlie guessed that was his way of saying hi.

"Where'd you play last year?" he asked.

"Played for the Downsview Eagles," he said.

Charlie shot a concerned look at Pudge. The Eagles played in the A division. The jump to AAA would be huge.

"The league was total garbage," Simon said. "My

parents forced me to play because the coach was a family friend. I told them no way I was going back. I think I got twenty shutouts — no kiddin'. When Mike told me about the Hawks, I accepted the offer."

Charlie pretended to be impressed. "That's incredible," he said. "Twenty shutouts in one season — you must have won the championship."

Simon spit on the ground. "The team totally choked. We lost in the semis to a team we'd beat like ten times during the regular season."

"Tough luck," Charlie said.

"Simon's gonna dominate," Mike said. "In fact, Alexi Tolstoy asked me about the team, and I told him to stay with the Snow Birds, unless he wanted to be backup."

Charlie knew Alexi was the best AAA goalie in the league — hands down. He couldn't believe what Mike was saying. Before he could reply, the bell rang and all the students began to shuffle to the front door.

"See you at the tryout," Charlie said.

Mike shrugged. "Later."

Simon thrust his chin out again and followed Mike.

Pudge put his hand on Charlie's shoulder, holding him back.

"What do you make of that?" Pudge said.

"Don't mind saying that I'm a bit freaked. Can you believe he told Alexi to get lost? Alexi's good enough to win a championship by himself."

"Mike's living in a dream world — always has. He thinks he's the next Sidney Crosby and can't understand why he never makes a good team. If his father wants to win — and from what I know about the guy he's competitive — then he'll want you on the Hawks."

They headed up the stairs to their lockers. Charlie slapped the railing.

"I'm totally spaced. I forgot about Matt. He turned down his spot on the Wildcats because he didn't want to play with Jake."

"That's a familiar song," Pudge said.

"I hear ya. I bet he'll be totally stoked about the Hawks. I'll talk to him today."

Pudge made a sour face. "Not so sure about Matt. He's been kind of busy lately."

Charlie waved him off. "This is hockey. He's got to play somewhere."

"I'll catch up with you," Pudge said. "Got to get to my locker before class."

He ran off. Charlie spotted another kid who'd been on the school team. He lived a block away from him on the same street. They weren't the closest friends, but he liked his serious-minded neighbour.

"Hey, Dylan. How's it going?"

"Not bad. Things are busy with hockey starting up. Did you figure out what you're gonna be doing?"

Charlie quickly filled him in on the Hawks. "I'm keeping my fingers crossed that some of the guys might switch over and we can play together, which would be totally awesome. Of course, that might not happen," he added.

"Not sure that's the best idea," Dylan said slowly. "Mike's not the easiest guy to deal with, and I don't think his father's any picnic either."

That made Charlie uneasy. Dylan never dissed people. "You're probably right about that. But I'm hoping the other guys will balance things out. Mike said his dad was committed to building things up and . . . we might go to tournaments and stuff . . ." He didn't know what else to say.

"Who's playing goal?" Dylan asked suddenly.

"Simon Godfrey."

It seemed that Dylan was trying hard not to laugh. "Good luck at the tryout," he said. "Tell me how it goes."

They said goodbye and Charlie went into his home-room as the bell sounded.

"How is Charlie doing today?"

"I'm good, Mr. Hilton," Charlie said. "Been busy working on the book report."

"Glad to hear it," Hilton said. "I'm looking forward to reading it."

Charlie took his seat and pulled out a folder. He'd worked all weekend on the report. His teacher hadn't thought too much of his first one, but this time he'd put in the effort. He flipped the pages, scanning anxiously for mistakes. He didn't want to let Hilton down again, not after the school tournament. He'd been the coach — and probably the best coach Charlie had ever had.

The crackle of the speaker interrupted him. The other students stood for the national anthem.

"Good morning, students. Would everyone please rise."

Charlie gave his report a final hopeful look and stood beside his desk.

3

COACH'S CORNER

Charlie glanced at the clock and groaned. The tryout started in ten minutes.

"I'm driving as fast as I can," his mother said. "We'll make it."

"We'll make it for the end of the tryout. I'm going to look like an idiot, being the last one on the ice."

"You won't look anything of the sort. We're here."

She pulled up to the front doors. Charlie raced to get his equipment from the trunk.

"Don't forget I'm working tonight," she called out. "Grandma is home. You'll need to walk back, or else catch a lift with someone."

He was in too much of a hurry to worry. "No problem, Mom," he said.

"Good luck, Charlie. Have fun."

He flew through the lobby and practically jumped an entire flight of stairs. The dressing rooms were at the end of a long corridor. As he approached, he could hear Mike's voice above the others.

"I gotta get some wingers with wheels," he said. "I don't want to be waiting for guys to catch up all the time."

Charlie didn't relish dressing in a room with Mike. He saw another dressing room was open and continued on. A huge grin spread across his face. He was greeted by one of the most awesome things he'd ever seen.

"Nice of you to join us," Pudge said.

Nick and Scott saluted on cue.

This was beyond his wildest dreams. He never thought Pudge, Nick or Scott would actually switch teams.

"You weren't going to tell me?" he managed.

"We thought you'd start crying," Scott said.

"You were probably right. What made you decide?"

An awkward silence followed. Finally, Pudge said, "We talked it over last night. You were right. This is a chance to play together. We might not get another—"

"Now *I'm* gonna start crying," Scott said.

They all laughed and began joking around as Charlie dressed hurriedly.

"Too bad Zachary didn't come," he said, pulling on his pants. "I can understand why he'd want to stay with the Snow Birds. But it would've been perfect if he was here."

"I called him. He agreed to think about it," Pudge said. "Not sure if it's possible, though, since he'll miss the first tryout."

Charlie could barely contain his enthusiasm. Even without Zachary it was amazing to have his three friends on the team. As he finished tying his skates, a man popped his head into the dressing room. He had thinning grey hair and a long face. Charlie thought he looked tired.

"The Zamboni is coming on the ice," he said.

"We'll start as soon as it's finished."

That gave Charlie a chance to look around the room. He recognized some of the players. Two guys he didn't know stuck out. One was retying a skate and the other was taping his shin pads, as if they'd done the same thing a thousand times.

Charlie did a double take when the boy tying his skate looked up. They were identical twins. Their likeness was almost freaky. The twin taping his shin pads caught him staring. Charlie cleared his throat a few times, trying to think of something to say.

"How are you guys doing?" he said finally. "I know most of the guys trying out, but I haven't met you before."

"I'm Christopher," the skate-tying twin said. "This is my brother Robert."

Charlie said hello, and then introduced his friends.

"So you look like you've played a bit of hockey," Charlie said after the introductions were over.

"We have," Robert said.

"Did you play last year?"

"Yup."

Not the most talkative pair, he thought.

"What team did you play on? I assume you were on the same team since you're wearing the same sweaters."

"We played for Watford," Robert said.

They even sounded the same, Charlie said to himself. He still couldn't tell them apart.

"They're a double-A team, right?" Pudge said. "Pretty good one too, if memory serves."

"We won the championship last year," Robert said, "so I guess we had a decent team."

Charlie was encouraged. That was the longest reply yet. He decided to focus on Robert. He seemed the more outgoing of the two.

"So Robert, what school do you go to?"

"We go to Flemington."

Charlie and his friends exchanged looks. Terrence Falls had beaten Flemington in a shootout in the semi-finals of the tournament. Charlie had scored to tie it up in the last seconds.

The twins started laughing.

"We don't want to talk about that game," Robert said.

"No question we got lucky," Charlie said. He dug his gloves out of his bag. "So what positions do you play?" he asked. "Would you happen to be a defence pair?"

Christopher and Robert both smiled. "We've always played D together, ever since novice," Robert said.

"Awesome," Charlie said. "This team could use defencemen. Right now it looks like we're stuck with those two clowns." He pointed at Scott and Nick.

"Just because I have a shiny red nose, long frizzy hair, and size thirty shoes doesn't mean I'm a clown," Scott said.

"Actually, it does," Nick said.

Scott smacked his forehead with his hand. "No wonder people are always laughing at me." He turned to the twins. "Do either of you have a banana cream pie? I need to throw one at Nick."

The twins looked bewildered. Charlie started to laugh, as did most of the others. Christopher and Robert soon joined in.

"I had pie," Robert said, "but I left it in my dad's car."

Charlie was about to make a joke about his mother's cookies when the door swung open. The handle smashed into the wall. Tom Dunn entered. He dropped a large cardboard box to the floor, then clapped his hands loudly a few times.

"Great to see you all. We're going to have a great team — a powerhouse. This is the start of a new dynasty in this league, and you can quote me on that. You wait and see. I hope some of you guys are good enough to make the grade. It'll be intense. It'll be tough. But it'll be fun too — cause we're going to win, and win big."

He proceeded to ask each player his name and position, and where he played the year before. He got to Charlie.

"And you?"

"Charlie Joyce. I'm a forward. I just moved to Terrence Falls."

He frowned and wrote something on his clipboard. "I believe we met. And Mike mentioned your name. There are three forwards in hockey. Which one do you play?" he said gruffly.

"Centre, I guess."

"Do you guess, or do you know?" Dunn said harshly.

Charlie was taken aback. "Usually I play centre, but I'll play anywhere."

He grunted and moved on. When he finished, he reached down and ripped the box open, pulling out a pile of hockey sweaters. He held one up. Charlie was impressed. A fierce-looking hawk was emblazoned on the front, with *Terrence Falls Hawks* written underneath in small lettering.

"Nice practice sweaters, or what? I want my team to look sharp. You win by doing things right — and that means first class. So take off what you're wearing and put on one of these." He tossed a jersey to each player. "Obviously I don't know your skill levels, except for a few boys I've seen before, so I've divided you arbitrarily into two groups, white and red. Don't worry about who's on your team at this point. I'll be making some cuts today, and then some more after the next tryout."

Charlie and Pudge got white sweaters. Scott, Nick and the twins were red. Charlie put his on. Dunn wasn't kidding about first class. These were top of the line. He could only imagine what they cost.

The older man popped his head into the room again. "Mr. Dunn, the Zamboni is off. Should I tell the boys in the other room to go on?"

"Sure, and get your skates on and get out there," Dunn said. The door closed. "I want to see big-time effort," he said to the players. "We don't have much time for tryouts. The first regular season game is in ten days. So give everything you got. Don't be afraid to get physical, either. I only played one way — intense and tough. Hockey's not a game for scared little boys. But I don't have to tell you guys that. I know you have the right stuff. I can sense these things. I can tell just by looking at a player whether or not he has the jam to go into the corner and fight for the puck."

He looked around the room, nodding at each player as if to prove it.

The door flew open. Mike had bodychecked it with his shoulder.

"Ice is ready. Let's get ready to rumble, ladies."

His father clapped his hands a few times.

"Head on out. I just have to strap on the ol' blades. Take a few laps and warm up."

Charlie filed onto the ice behind the others.

"I guess we know who's coaching," he said to Pudge, as they skated slowly around the rink.

* * *

They spent a few minutes circling the ice and shooting on the goalies before Dunn blasted his whistle and waved the players in.

"Drop to a knee, boys."

Behind him, the older man struggled across the ice, his ankles turned inwards, burdened by a large pail of pucks and a stack of orange pylons. Some of the players laughed openly. Charlie didn't. He felt sorry for the guy. He certainly didn't look happy.

"I'm sure most of you know me already — or at least you know my stores — Dunn's Sportsmart. My name's Tom Dunn. I'm your coach and sponsor. And the nice thing about a sponsor who owns twenty sporting goods stores is the top-of-the-line equipment! I'll be outfitting the team with new gear from head to toe. As well, all team members get a twenty-five-percent discount on anything they buy in-store. Twenty-five's the best I can do — gotta make a little money."

He laughed heartily.

"On the ice, I'm Coach Dunn, and I'm looking forward to working with those of you who make the team. I became successful by demanding excellence, from myself and from the people who work for me. I'm tough, but fair. You perform, put in the effort, and nobody will treat you better than me."

The older man had dropped the pucks and pylons at the bench and tottered over to centre.

Dunn gestured towards him. "This here is Edward Shaw — Coach Shaw to you. He's our manager and assistant coach. He manages my Terrence Falls store. He's a great guy and a great hockey man. We also have a trainer. He's sitting up in the stands." Dunn pointed to a lone figure. "That's Todd. Let's have a massive 'Hello Todd!' to make him feel welcome."

Charlie mumbled a quiet hello, as did a few others. Mike, Simon and the players kneeling around them screamed theirs. Todd's head jerked up. He waved a book, and began reading again.

"Let's get down to business. First, some skating drills, then we'll introduce the pucks. After that we scrimmage — red versus white. Full contact. Now, everyone to the far boards."

4

TRYING TIMES

Charlie kicked at the ice as he waited behind the net for Dunn to announce the next drill.

"Give me Red on the line. Skate hard to the other end, touch the boards with your stick and come back. Go!"

Nick led the field on the way down, Scott and the twins following not far behind. Mike trailed all four — but he stopped well short of the boards, then flicked his stick half-heartedly, which gave him a big lead, and he was the first one back.

"Way to bring it, Mikey," Dunn said. He slapped his stick on the ice a few times. "That's what I'm lookin' for. White, show me what you got." He blew his whistle.

Charlie dug his blades into the ice, taking short, choppy strides. As he neared the goal line, Charlie turned sideways and allowed his skate to slide. He timed his stop perfectly, going only as close to the boards as he needed to touch them with his stick. The sound of his skates carving crisply into the ice spurring him on, Charlie was first back by ten feet. Pudge came in second.

"Listen up, boys," Dunn said. "This next one's

tricky. Skate hard to the blue line. Lower one knee to the ice, stand back up, and then lower the other. Alternate knees the length of the ice. Make sure each knee hits. Mikey, why don't you have a go to demonstrate."

"Yeah, baby!" Mike whooped, and he set off.

Charlie knew this drill was difficult, especially towards the end when your legs got tired. He was curious to see how Mike would do.

Mike slowed noticeably on the way back, looking unsteady as he bobbed up and down. Ten feet inside the blue line, he lost his balance, but instead of stopping he tried to switch knees again and ended up falling.

A few of the players laughed. Mike's face was beet red, and he looked down at his skates.

"Be quiet," Dunn said. "Red, get going."

Charlie watched with concern as most of the Red players spun around, crashed into each other, or fell. The only ones who bothered touching their knees to the ice on the way back were his friends and the twins. When it was their turn, he and Pudge were first back again.

"We're going to switch it up," Dunn said. "I need Red in one corner and White in the other. This is called the one-on-one challenge. I'll blow the whistle and the first two players skate around each circle, and then head for the puck at centre. The first player takes it on a breakaway. Second guy tries to stop him."

"I want you to go hard. Full contact. I'm looking for players with the guts to really go for it. Coach Shaw, can we have the pucks at centre?"

Mike was first up for Red. Dunn brought the whistle to his lips. Mike took off, as the other player hesitated, uncertain. Dunn blew the whistle, but by then Mike was halfway around the first circle, and was way in front when he picked up the puck at centre.

Ten feet out he faked a backhand, brought it across to his forehand, and tried to flip the puck in on the glove side. The goalie hadn't budged, and butterflied to his left, smothering the puck easily. Charlie was impressed by the goalie's quickness.

Simon had taken over goal by the time Charlie's turn came up. Better than Alexi Tolstoy? He'd see about that. But he had to win the race first, he reminded himself. The whistle blew and he was off like a shot. He needn't have bothered. His opponent was slow at best, and Charlie won by twenty feet. Once he crossed the blue line he expected Simon to come out to challenge. Instead, he stayed way back in his net, almost on the goal line. This was supposed to be the number-one goalie? At the hash marks, with the entire net to shoot at, Charlie snapped a wrist shot, stick side, to the bottom right corner. Simon barely moved.

On Charlie's next turn, the first goalie was back in net. He'd done well, stopping most of the breakaways. Charlie skated hard and was ten feet ahead when he gathered the puck up. He slowed at the top of the circle. The goalie was in front of his crease and he couldn't shoot with him so far out. He decided on his favourite move — one he'd practised endlessly with his dad in their backyard rink. His dad would put a plank of wood across the lower half of the net, and Charlie had to backhand the puck into the net from various distances. Over time he'd learned to flip it almost straight up under the crossbar from in close.

He threw in a token forehand move to keep the goalie honest, and then drove hard on his backhand to the goalie's glove side. The goalie dropped his left pad against the post and held up his glove. The corner was still exposed, and Charlie thought he could sneak it in. Five feet from the net he dipped his left shoulder and bent his knee for leverage.

Next thing he knew, Charlie was flat on his back sliding into the boards. The trailing player hadn't quit, and dove to knock the puck away. Charlie was able to absorb the impact with his right skate. The other player was sliding head first and only managed to spin himself around at the last second to avoid hitting the boards straight on.

"Are you okay?" Charlie said, worried that he'd really hurt himself. "You came out of nowhere." The player struggled to his knees.

"Banged my shoulder," he gasped.

"Maybe you're winded," Charlie said. "Take it slow and wait till your breath comes back." The player nodded and slowed his breathing.

Dunn's whistle blasted several times. "Keep moving. You're holding up the drill," Dunn said, skating over. He narrowed his eyes and stared at Charlie.

"He hit the boards real hard," Charlie said, "and I . . ."

"He's hurt — not your problem," Dunn said. "Leave that to the trainer. I want my players to have a killer instinct. Don't wait around. Keep going. Why'd you slow down? You should've scored." He reached down and pulled the injured player to his feet. The player winced and held his shoulder.

"Suck it up, kid," Dunn said gruffly. "Hockey's a tough game. Don't quit because of a little bruise. Back in line, both of you."

They started back.

"Are you sure you're all right?" Charlie said.

He could see the player was fighting back tears, and Charlie didn't blame him. It was a hard hit.

"I'm fine," he said. "I just need to catch my breath."

Charlie didn't believe him. "You should sit out the rest of this drill," he said.

They joined their respective lines. After a few more players Dunn blew his whistle, so Charlie didn't get another chance.

"Time for the scrimmage, boys," Dunn said. "That was good hustle. White, you're with Coach Shaw. Red, you stay with me. I'll also be reffing. Game rules: full contact, offsides, icing — the works."

Shaw held the door open and the White players shuffled onto the bench. Charlie filed in with the others. He was about to sit down when he felt a tap on his shoulder.

"I told Mr. Dunn that I've barely seen a game," Coach Shaw whispered. "He appointed me manager, but I didn't think I'd have to do any coaching. You look like you know a lot about hockey. Could you help organize? How many players at a time?"

Charlie assumed he was joking and was about to laugh. Then he saw how distraught the man was.

"Don't worry about it, Coach Shaw. I'll put the guys into lines."

"Thanks," he said gratefully. "Here's a list of names."

He handed Charlie a clipboard.

Charlie felt weird acting like the coach. "Listen up. Coach Shaw asked me to sort out the lines." They all looked at him strangely. He only knew two guys. "Samuel and Richard, you should be one defence pair. Do we have any other defencemen?" Two guys held up their hands. "I guess you'll be the other pair." He counted the remaining players. "That leaves eight forwards, which means we have to go with two centres and three sets of wingers. The centres will get more ice time, but what else can we do?"

No one said a word, so Charlie continued.

"How many centres do we have?"

Again, no one answered.

"I can play centre, but we still need another."

Dunn blew his whistle. "Edward, what's the hold up? Get your players organized already. This ain't the Stanley Cup playoffs."

"Right with you, Mr. Dunn," Shaw stammered.

Charlie pointed at a player he'd noticed in the drills. Not the smoothest skater, but he seemed comfortable with the puck. "What's your name?"

"Jonathon."

"Can you help us out at centre?"

He agreed, and Charlie quickly paired up the wingers. He asked Jonathon to start, and the first line jumped the boards. He turned to his coach. "The defencemen can shift themselves," he said. "Maybe you could do the forwards." Shaw stared at him.

"Open the door for the guys coming off," Charlie said, and pointed to the forwards' door.

Shaw looked truly miserable, but dutifully took his

position by the door. Charlie sat next to Pudge.

"What do you think so far?" Pudge asked him quietly.

"Bit bizarre. I don't think Coach Shaw's ever seen a game in his life. We'll know better after the scrimmage. Apart from the twins, the talent level's not quite what I had hoped."

"Not much time to throw a team together," Pudge said. "I bet some more guys will come to the next tryout."

"If Matt comes out, we'll be good. On D, we got Scott and Nick, and the twins. You and I can be together on one line, and that Jonathon guy is not bad. A few more players and we got an okay lineup."

They watched the action. After a minute Jonathon headed to the bench.

"Centre," he yelled, holding his stick over his head.

"I guess I'm up," Charlie said, hopping over the boards.

5

THINK FAST

The door swung open. Scott and Nick walked in, followed by Pudge. Charlie had been waiting for his friends at his mom's café for over half an hour.

"C-man. What's shakin'?" Nick said.

"Not much. Just waiting for you slugs."

"Sorry for being late," Pudge said. He cast an accusing eye at Scott. "We got a slow start."

"No worries," Charlie said. "We don't have too much time before the tryout, though."

"I'm the guilty party," Scott said. "But I had important business."

"This'll be good," Nick said.

"It is good," he affirmed. "I was on a conference call with the President of the United States and . . ." He looked around the café. "I've said too much already. Let's just say the world is now a safer place; and don't bother thanking me. I do it because I care."

"How are the boys doing?" Charlie's mom said. She peered at them from behind the counter.

"We're doing well, Mrs. Joyce," Pudge said.

She sighed. "Pudge, as refreshing as it is to see a young man with good manners, you make me feel old when you call me Mrs. Joyce. I told you before — it's Donna."

Pudge flushed. "Okay, Mrs. Joyce. I'll try."

She laughed. "I know you have a tryout soon, but would anyone like a snack?"

"I supposed I could take a run at your world-famous smoked turkey sandwich," Scott said.

"Salad with that?"

"Why not? Saving the world gives a guy an appetite you wouldn't believe."

His friends laughed.

"You got it. Anyone else?" No one replied. "Shirley, one ST with side salad."

"Gotcha," Shirley replied from the kitchen.

"I believe a humongous sandwich is what most professional athletes eat just before a game," Nick said.

"Doesn't matter what I eat, playing against most of the guys who tried out yesterday," Scott said. "We could all eat a cow and still make this team."

His joke was met with silence. He was right. The talent level was too low for AAA.

"Maybe I can help."

Charlie gasped. Zachary stood at the door and winked at his friends.

Everyone began talking at once.

"Hold on a sec," Scott said over the noise. "Let's make one thing clear. I'm not sharing my sandwich with Zachary."

Zachary sat down at the table. "I got to thinking. Like Charlie said, the Snow Birds are stacked, and ice time will be scarce. My dad called Dunn last night and he said I could try out. I figured I'd play a ton with the

Hawks — and keep you guys out of trouble."

Zachary's arrival lifted all their spirits and they joked around as usual all the way to the arena. Charlie laughed at everything; he couldn't help himself. His dream team was actually happening. Three days ago he wasn't going to be able to play at all. Now he was playing AAA with all his friends.

* * *

When they got to the rink, Charlie noticed the Hawks only had one dressing room.

"Looks like we're all in room seven," Charlie said. "I wonder why we're all together?"

"Guess the coach is trying to foster team spirit," Scott said.

They walked down the stairs and along the narrow corridor leading to the dressing rooms. Charlie went in first. He saw a large pile of cardboard boxes at the far end of the room, with dozens of sticks leaning against them. The players were sitting quietly, still in street clothes.

Charlie sat next to Christopher and Robert. "Why aren't we getting ready?"

Robert shrugged. "Coach Shaw told us to sit tight and wait. That was ten minutes ago." Charlie counted the players in the room: fifteen skaters plus two goalies, Simon and the kid who'd impressed him last tryout, Martin. "Where are the rest of the guys?" he said.

"Your guess is as good as mine," Christopher said.

Zachary caught his eye. "What's the story?"

"Coach told us to chill," Charlie said.

"Why?"

"No clue."

They didn't have long to wait. The next moment the door flung open. Mike stormed in, followed by his father and Coach Shaw.

Mike walked to the back, grabbed a stick, banged it on the floor a few times, and then leaned on it to test the flex.

"You're in trouble now, Simon. You won't even see the pucks when I fire them at you with this howitzer."

"That's not fair, dude. You already got a rocket," Simon said seriously.

Mike laughed. "Life's not fair, Si. Let's get out there and start shootin', Dad."

"Hold on a minute, Mike," Dunn said. "Sit down and let me talk to the team."

"Cool," he said, flexing the stick again.

"Boys, I'm a guy that makes quick decisions. I go with my gut. That's what's taken me to the top in the business world." He paused to look the players over. "I made the cuts last night. I saw the players I liked. The guys who didn't measure up . . ." He shrugged. "Too bad for them. You wanna play elite hockey, you gotta have passion. Some of the guys I cut were good players — talented, solid skaters."

He thumped his fist to his chest. "What didn't they have, Mikey?"

"Heart. They got no heart."

"Good answer. Hockey's about guts, second effort, intimidation, being tougher than the other guy. Hit 'em first, I always say. We're going to punish the other teams, make them afraid to even come out on the ice. Wear 'em down and crush 'em — that's Hawks hockey. Remember that and we'll get along just fine. If you forget it, you'll get to know a little friend of mine named The Bench."

He crossed the room to where Mike was standing.

"Check this out, boys."

Dunn ripped a box open and pulled out a pair of hockey pants. Then he opened a few other boxes and pulled out shoulder, elbow and shin pads, and finally a pair of gloves. He tossed each piece of equipment on the floor. "Only the best for the Hawks. This is top-of-the-line — what the pros wear. Pick out what you need from each box. Most of the stuff is youth medium or large, but I brought some extra stuff so you shouldn't have any problems with sizing."

Charlie felt like a kid in a candy store as he pulled pants, shin pads, elbow pads, and shoulder pads from the various boxes. Dunn had emptied a big box with all the gloves on the floor. He picked up a pair. The palm was incredibly soft. He'd never had new equipment before, at least not this quality. His mother and father could never afford it. He put on the gloves and went over to Pudge.

"Is this not awesome?"

"Pretty dope," Pudge said. He held up a shin pad. "The protection's amazing, and they're light as a feather."

"I guess there are some benefits to having a coach who owns sporting goods stores."

"Stand in awe, boys," Scott said. He wore his new shoulder and elbow pads, and flexed his arms like a bodybuilder. "The first guy I hit will be going through the boards."

"You still have to catch the guy," Nick said. He gave the pads a whack with his hand.

"Didn't even feel it," Scott said. "Maybe you should start working out, Nick."

Charlie got dressed. He'd always been a little envious of guys who got to wear the best equipment. Now it was his turn. He was dying to get out on the ice. He could see the others felt the same way. Who wouldn't? The equipment made him feel invincible.

"Everyone satisfied?" Dunn said.

The players whooped their approval.

Dunn slapped a few players on the back. "Today, just wear your own helmets. This week you'll all come to the store and we'll measure you for new ones. We need to fit them exactly, with the right cage. If we tried to do it now, we'd never get to practise. And we're here to play hockey — right?"

He got an even louder yell this time.

"Help yourselves to two sticks each. They're all composites — the best. We got Eastons and Bauers."

Shaw coughed nervously. "Excuse me, Mr. Dunn. We didn't have enough Bauers in stock, so I brought these." He held a stick up.

Dunn snorted in disgust. "Why'd you bring that junk?" He shrugged. "Sorry, boys. I'll bring some more sticks next practice. Just grab an Easton or one of the quality Bauers." He turned to Shaw. "Call the Richmond store. They just got a shipment."

Shaw nodded and scribbled a note in a small black notebook.

"One last thing," Dunn said, "before we get out there." He held a purple hockey sweater with red trim. On the front a large, menacing hawk gripped a broken hockey stick in its claws. Dunn pointed to a white C stitched to the sweater. Dunn flipped it around — number 8. Charlie suppressed a gasp. That was his number — he'd worn it since novice and for the school team. Dunn had barely paid any attention to him — he'd been kind of mean, if anything. Maybe Mike or one of the other guys had talked to him. He would have preferred a team vote, but it was still a huge honour.

"So who wants this one?" Dunn said.

In spite of himself, Charlie felt a smile cross his face, and he reached out his hand. Dunn tossed the jersey across the room to Mike.

"You ready to lead this team to the championship?"

"Not a problem," Mike said.

Charlie felt like an idiot. He hoped no one had noticed. Of course Mike was captain. He'd go for number nine — lots of famous players had worn that.

Dunn held each sweater up, and a player wanting that number raised his hand. If two players wanted the same sweater, Dunn decided, usually telling the losing player to "get over it." When nine came up, Charlie held up his hand. Dunn didn't even look his way.

"Sean, nine's a goal scorer's number — it's got your name on it."

Sean was Mike's friend. Charlie breathed deeply — only a number, he reminded himself. He changed his strategy. This time he'd wait for a number no one wanted. He had to wait until everyone else picked, however. Zachary got his customary 15. Pudge got 5. Scott was 16 and Nick 17. They didn't look happy. Dunn held up 18. He felt ridiculous, the only guy without a sweater. He held up his hand and Dunn fired it over. At least it had an eight!

"Okay, you lazy slobs. How about we actually play some hockey? Finish dressing and hustle out. Edward, I want these boxes broken down and back in the van, then I want you on the ice too."

Shaw nodded glumly. He slowly started folding the boxes, so they would lie flat.

"And don't forget to get your new sticks," Dunn said. "Edward, leave the boxes for a sec and cut the sticks to whatever size they want."

Charlie was close to the sticks. He grabbed one of the Eastons. He'd flexed a few high-end composites in a hockey store — now he actually had one! Probably cost five times more than his stick. He waited in line for the assistant coach to cut the stick to size. Pudge came over.

"Impressive gear, or what?" Charlie said.

Pudge didn't answer right away. He raised his eyebrows and nodded a few times. Charlie could tell he wasn't happy about something.

"What's up?" he said.

Pudge shrugged. "The equipment is great — it's the best there is. I'm just thinkin' about school stuff. I'm cool."

Charlie left it alone. Pudge obviously didn't want to talk about it. It probably had nothing to do with the Hawks. How could it? All together on one team, best gear in the world, three hundred dollar sticks. How much better did it get?

SNEAK ATTACK

Charlie pulled his collar tightly around his neck to keep the rain from running down his back. School had just finished, and he was waiting for Matt. Matt had missed homeroom, the only class they had together, and Charlie hadn't seen him the rest of the day. Come to think of it, he hadn't seen him around much at all lately.

Finally, Charlie caught sight of him running out the doors.

"Hey, Matt!" he said.

Matt didn't stop. Instead, he sprinted off down the street. Charlie groaned and took off after him. Ten minutes standing in the pouring rain and now he was going for a jog! Charlie screamed his name several times. Finally, Matt turned around.

"Didn't know you could run like that," Charlie said, breathing heavily. "You should go for track this spring."

Matt didn't laugh. He looked at his watch. "I'm a little late for something. Sorry, but I gotta get going."

"I just wanted to fill you in on the Hawks."

The rain continued to pour down. Matt ran his hand across his face. "I don't know about that. It's been kinda crazy for me. School's intense. Don't care about hockey so much at the moment. Maybe I'll get back into it next year . . ." He broke off and looked at his watch again.

Charlie's mind flooded with questions. This wasn't the Matt he knew. Since when did he not care about hockey? What was the big hurry? And since when did he wear a watch? Charlie had to get to the bottom of it

"Why were you so late leaving school? I nearly caught pneumonia waiting for you."

"I didn't get my book report done for English. Hilton made me stay after school to finish it. I'll see you tomorrow."

Charlie was even more bewildered now. Matt was a straight-A student. He never missed an assignment.

"Hold on. What've you been up to? You missed the first tryout, and the team's been picked. I could speak to the coach. You should see the equipment we got — it's unreal. Easton composite sticks, pro gloves, just incredible stuff."

"That sounds great, Charlie. But I don't feel like playing. No big deal. I appreciate you telling me and calling . . . I'm just busy."

"Busy doing what?"

He shrugged. "Got a job, which is why I'm in a hurry. It starts in ten minutes, and my boss said I'd better not be late again or he'd take it out of my pay."

"Where are you working?"

"With a roofing company. I help rip the shingles."

"You'd rather work than play hockey?"

"Some of us don't have a choice." His tone had an edge to it. He looked at his watch again. "I really gotta go. I'll catch up with you later. Good luck with the—"

"Roscoe, let me introduce you to the two biggest losers in Terrence Falls."

The voice filled Charlie with dread. Jake was crossing the street towards them with his buddies, Liam and Thomas. The big new kid was with him too.

"Great," Matt growled. "Now I'm definitely going to be late."

"You can get going," Charlie said. "I'll tell these guys to buzz."

Matt folded his arms across his chest, his eyes narrowing.

"We really miss seeing you around, Matt," Liam said. "You run off after school every day. I wonder why."

Jake had a big grin on his face.

"We gotta go," Charlie said. "We've got no time for this. Bye."

"Why the hurry?" Jake sneered. "Oh, I forgot. Matt's gotta make some cash for his old man. How's the roofing business?"

Liam and Thomas snickered. Matt flushed and balled his fists.

"Did I tell you boys that Matt's dad is doing some yard work for my dad?" Jake continued. "My dad got him a few other jobs too. I think he's cleaning out our garage. Didn't do a good job raking our leaves — missed a few — but I let him off the hook. I even gave him a two-buck tip."

"Maybe it'll be enough for Matt to buy a lollipop," Liam said.

"Or a bag of chips," Thomas said.

Charlie didn't understand. Why would Matt's dad rake leaves for Jake?

"We gotta go, so later," Charlie said.

Jake stepped closer. "Joyce, I understand you're trying out for Dunn's new team. What's it called?"

"The Hawks," Liam said.

"With the guys on that team, they should call it the Flops," Roscoe said.

Jake laughed and gave Roscoe a high-five. "It'll be fun when we play you. You might learn something — like the meaning of pain." He lunged forward and punched Charlie's shoulder with his palm.

It hurt, but Charlie didn't show it. He moved back, keeping his eye on Jake.

Thomas chuckled. "We promise to take it easy when it's 10–0 after the first period."

"Matt, you didn't show for the Wildcats practices. I hope our little fight at the tournament didn't scare you off," Jake said.

"Dudes, look. I think Matt's crying," Liam said.

"I'd be crying too if my dad was such a loser," Jake said.

Matt's face was so pale Charlie thought he might be sick. Matt didn't react to Jake's taunting, however. That surprised him, since Matt had a temper. Why would he just take this from Jake?

Charlie wasn't about to let Jake get away with it.

"I guess you all think you're being tough, but this act is beyond lame. Without Matt, you'll be lucky to make the playoffs. Just watch — it'll be the Hawks vs the Snow Birds for the championship."

"Listen to that," Liam howled. He was bent over

laughing. "The dude's delusional."

"The dude's pathetic," Roscoe said.

"The dude's a dead man," Jake said.

He lunged at Charlie again. This time Charlie was ready and blocked Jake's punch. He followed up with a double forearm to Jake's chest.

Jake fell back a few steps. "Guys, get a shovel, 'cause by the time I'm finished with this guy you'll have to scrape him off the sidewalk."

"Take him down, Jake," Thomas said.

"Hammer time," Liam said.

Charlie circled to his right.

"Here's an interesting situation," Charlie heard someone say.

He lowered his fists and relaxed. His friends had appeared out of nowhere.

"Why can't you little boys behave?" Scott continued.

"Don't you know four against two is not a fair fight?" Nick growled, looking straight at Jake.

Pudge placed his hands on his hips and stood next to Charlie.

"You guys just finished choir practice?" Jake said. "Or were you doing flower arrangements after school again?"

"Doesn't Hilton teach that class?" Liam asked.

"You're a tough talker when Hilton's not around," Charlie shot back.

"I forgot," Jake said. "Joyce is in love with the great Hilton. Sorry for not dropping to my knees and praying to that jerk. One day maybe you'll be lucky enough to play for a real coach."

"One day maybe you'll be lucky enough to play for a real team," Charlie said.

Jake twisted his mouth to the side. "Have your fun now, Joyce. It won't be fun when the Wildcats beat the Hawks to a pulp. Let's space, dudes."

They crossed the street. Jake turned around. He pointed two fingers to his eyes, and then at Charlie. "Matt, tell your old man he can clean our toilets tomorrow," he said.

He and his friends laughed uproariously.

"I'm going to crush that guy when we play against the Wildcats," Scott said. "He's going through the boards, I swear it."

"What was that all about?" Pudge asked Charlie.

"Don't know exactly. Me and Matt were just talking and they come up and started messing with us. No reason. Right, Matt?"

Matt didn't reply. He looked dejectedly at his watch.

"Typical Jake — chickens out once the numbers aren't on his side. Never one for a fair fight," Nick said.

"We owe you guys," Charlie said. "Lucky for us you showed up."

"You could take them, easy," Pudge said. "They're full of hot air, that's all."

Charlie sighed. "Something tells me I'll get the chance to test that theory. What's Jake's problem anyway?"

"He was the best hockey player in school — until you came," Pudge said.

"I'm not sure about that," he replied. He didn't want Pudge saying that in front of the guys. "There's a screw missing in his head, that's all I know."

"We were on the way to my dad's for dinner," Pudge said. "You want to come?"

"I'm not gonna pass up a chance to scarf at Bruno's Bistro," Charlie laughed. "Can we cruise by my house first, so I can drop off my knapsack and tell my mom? It's right on the way."

"No problem," Pudge said. "You up for it, Matt?"

"Thanks, but I gotta go. I'm really late now." He turned to Charlie. "Sorry about that. It's a weird situation . . . I have to be more careful . . . and . . . I gotta go. Bye."

He ran off down the street.

Charlie cupped his hands around his mouth. "I'll call you later," he yelled.

He turned to face his friends. "Does anyone have a clue what's going on with Matt? He said he was working for a roofing company — and that he's not going to play hockey. Jake was also saying some random stuff about Matt's dad. Pudge, you know anything?"

Pudge didn't answer at first. He looked uncomfortable. Then he said, "I know Matt's job is taking up a lot of time. Maybe he wants to focus on school the rest of the time."

"He's the smartest kid in school as it is. He could cut his marks in half and they'd still be higher than mine," Scott said.

Pudge was the type of guy who always seemed to have the inside story. Charlie had a feeling he knew more. "You got any info?" he persisted.

"It's not really for me to say," Pudge said.

"We can't help if we don't know," Charlie said. "And it seems like Matt could use some help."

Pudge nodded. "You know most of it, so you may as well get the rest of the story. My dad told me yesterday. Matt's dad worked for the same building company for years. He's a carpenter. The company closed down in the summer, and he hasn't been able to find a new job. I understand the family's hurting financially . . . and, well, Matt's trying to help out."

"So that's why he's working for the roofers and that's why there's no time for hockey. He's also messing up at school," Charlie said. "Hilton kept him after class to finish his book report."

They turned the corner onto Charlie's street.

"Is Matt's dad a good carpenter?" he asked Pudge.

"My dad told me he did an awesome job for him at the restaurant a few years ago," Pudge said. "Built an entire set of cabinets in, like, two days."

"My mom's been saying she needs a ton of stuff for the café. I could put her in touch with Matt's dad."

"We should all ask around," Pudge said. "Maybe we can drum up some business for him."

"Good idea," Charlie said. "Ask anyone you know — parents, relatives, friends — anything's better than yard work for Jake!"

Pudge snapped his fingers. "Why don't I see if I can get Matt a job at the restaurant? He'd make good money, and pick his own hours too, like only work on weekends."

"Which would leave time for hockey and school," Charlie said. "I definitely need to speak to Dunn about Matt. If this works, and Matt's available to play, I'm sure he'll give him a spot."

"Worth a try," Nick said.

"Gentlemen, prepare to be amazed by my blazing speed," Scott said.

He took off towards Charlie's house. His friends followed in hot pursuit. Charlie usually relished these little challenges, but this time he was too preoccupied by Matt's situation to enjoy the race. Matt must be feeling humiliated. If Jake ever said anything like that about his dad, Charlie didn't know what he'd do. And the idea of Matt not playing hockey was impossible. He had to try to help him — but was there really anything he could do?

Why were things always so complicated?

7

LINE CHANGE

"Let's go, driver. What's the hold-up?"

The team bus jerked forward at Dunn's command, and slowly pulled out of the parking lot. "Listen up," Dunn said. He stood next to the driver, facing the players. "I'm gonna call out the lineup for today's game. After I'm done, I want you to move so you're sitting with your linemates or defence partner."

Charlie expected Mike to be centre on the first line, so it was no surprise to hear his name called first. Then Dunn announced Zachary and Pudge as his wingers.

Pudge elbowed Charlie. "Is this for real?" he whispered. "I figured our line would be together."

What could he say? "Season's just started. Probably going to try a bunch of different line combos."

"Second line — Sean is the pivot, with Jacob and Wesley on the flanks . . ."

Charlie pushed back into his seat. He was on the third line — the third line!

Dunn dropped his clipboard onto his seat. "It's about a thirty-minute drive to the Tornadoes' rink," he said. "I wanna hear some hockey talk. Figure out what you're gonna do on the ice. Work out some plays. I'll give you ten minutes, and then I'll pull out the white-board for a strategy session."

Charlie dug his fingernails into the armrest. Third line — on *this* team!

"Move back, Joyce." Mike was standing in the aisle. "Pudge is on my line," he said.

"Okay . . . right," Charlie stammered. He felt as if everyone on the bus was looking at him. To make things worse, he didn't even hear Dunn call out his line. Was he even centre? He stood to let Mike sit next to Pudge and looked out the window, pretending to see something interesting. He'd let everyone else find his seat, and then he could figure out where he was supposed to sit.

"Hey, Charlie. Over here."

Jonathon waved and pointed at an empty seat next to him. Charlie sat down, grateful for the invitation, but still reeling from being put on the third line.

"I think we were on the white team together, for the tryout," Charlie said. "You and me played centre. I'm Charlie Joyce."

Jonathon shook Charlie's hand warmly. "I know. And I feel weird that I'm supposed to be centre. You played centre on the school team, right?"

Charlie nodded.

"I was at the tournament final — awesome game. And you played great. We should've won."

"Thanks. It went down to the wire. I still can't believe how it ended."

"The whole team was bogus!" Sean glared at Charlie from where he was sitting, a couple of rows in front. "Chelsea totally dominated us. Hilton is clueless.

He made the most stupid, brain-dead cuts from the team, and it was his fault we lost. He cut me after the first tryout, and Mike too! Totally lame."

It was on the tip of his tongue to fire back that Hilton's mistake was even letting Sean and Mike try out. Instead, Charlie said diplomatically, "Picking a team's tough, especially when there isn't much time. Hilton even said that he may have made some mistakes."

"Tell me about it," Sean fumed. "Doesn't matter now anyway. We need to focus on this season, and not some bogus high school tournament." He turned around and settled back into his seat.

Jonathon rolled his eyes and nodded towards Sean. Charlie had to force himself not to laugh.

Charlie's other linemate leaned across the aisle. "Hey, guys. I'm David Simpson. Right wing on your line." He paused and continued in a whisper. "I was cut after the first tryout for the school team too, but I deserved it." He started laughing, which set Charlie and Jonathon off.

Sean glared at Charlie again. "I can tell you guys are thinking about the game like Coach told us! Time to get serious. I want to win this game — big time. We need to establish our rep early. The Tornadoes finished last in the league last year. Our first two lines are totally stacked. You guys on the third line need to make sure you don't blow it and give up cheap goals. It'll be 5–0 before the first — that is, if you guys focus."

"I don't know about that," Charlie said. "We weren't even in the league last year, and we've hardly practised. Besides, for a lot of guys this is their first triple-A game. I think we're in for a serious battle."

"First triple-A game!" Sean said. "You and your friends are all up on yourselves because you played triple-A last year. The rest of us can play too, dude. You guys act like you invented the game."

"That's not it at all. I didn't say me . . . I mean . . . what I meant was . . ."

"Hey, Mike," Sean called. "Joyce thinks we're gonna lose today. Thinks we don't have enough talent, except for him and his buddies, of course."

"I didn't say that. Give me a break."

"Tell Mr. Superstar that he's on the third line for a reason," Mike said. "Just watch and learn, and maybe I'll let him touch the championship trophy."

Dunn poked his head around. "Joyce, I couldn't help hearing what you said. I will not accept defeat. I'm a winner, and so are my teams. If you're not that kind of player, you won't be around for too long."

Charlie gritted his teeth and kept quiet, staring intently at the back of the seat in front of him. He was too angry to speak. He was supposed to play with Mike and Sean? He'd rather pound them into the boards! Thankfully, Sean and Mike began a heated debate over who should be on the power play.

"Forget them," Jonathon said quietly. "You're twice the player either of them are, and they know it. That's really what it's all about."

"He totally twisted what I said."

"You don't have to convince me. Both of them are out of control — especially Mike. He wasn't that easy to deal with before this team. Now he thinks he's in the NHL."

"I guess we have to make the best of it," Charlie

said, glad for the sympathetic words.

"I'm under no illusions," Jonathon said. "Me and David were talking about it before we got on the bus. I admit I'm glad to try triple-A hockey — it'll be a learning experience — but I doubt I'll ever be more than an average player. I consider myself lucky to even get the chance. To play with you, on the same line, is awesome. I just hope I don't slow you down."

Charlie knew Jonathon worked hard and was unselfish with the puck. He wasn't the best player, but he contributed to the team.

"You're being hard on yourself. I thought you earned a spot on the team. Besides, the first game is always the toughest. Even if our line has some problems today, things will start clicking once we play together a few times."

"I'll take your word for it," he said. "By the way, I forgot, a mutual friend told me to say hi."

"Who's that?"

"Julia."

Charlie flushed slightly. He hoped Jonathon hadn't noticed. "Julia?"

"You know — Julia Chow."

Of course he knew her. Julia was in his homeroom class. She was also a terrific athlete, and had been captain of the girls junior hockey team in the school tournament. She was a very popular girl, had lots of friends, and was smart too. They'd spoken a few times, and for some reason a few of his friends liked to pretend there was a thing between them. He knew they were only teasing. Anyway, ever since he'd seen her hanging with Jake, he'd avoided talking to her.

"Of course — Julia," he said, as casually as he could manage. "How do you know her?"

"Next-door neighbour my whole life. She's like a sister — we practically grew up together. Anyway, she told me to say hi."

"Hi back, I guess."

Jonathon grinned. "I'll deliver the message."

They were interrupted by Dunn telling everyone to be quiet.

"Eyes front and centre, boys. Time to get serious. I wanna go over our forechecking. We're going to be the most aggressive team in the league, slam some bodies, force turnovers, and intimidate. That's Hawks hockey. So listen up and learn. First line will start, with Richard and Samuel on D."

What a contrast to Coach Hilton, Charlie thought, as he listened to Dunn drone on for the next twenty minutes. Hilton simplified the game, explaining everything so clearly that you knew exactly what to do. Dunn did the opposite. The whiteboard was soon covered in a confusing mass of lines, dots, and arrows going every which way, and Charlie had a hard time making sense of any of it. He stopped listening after five minutes — and wondered if Julia had really said hi.

8

TRIPLE-A FRAY

The referee dropped the puck. The Tornadoes centre easily won the draw to his right defenceman, who one-timed the puck across the ice to his defence partner. Zachary pressured, and the defenceman banked it off the boards.

"Be there, Mike," Charlie said, half-aloud. Centre was supposed to cover that zone. Instead, Mike stayed in the middle. The Tornadoes left winger picked it up on the fly and headed towards the Hawks' net.

At the blue line, the winger faked inside and swerved to the outside. Richard tried to stand him up; Charlie knew he prided himself on making big hits. The inside move caused him to lose his balance, however, and the player sidestepped the intended bone-crusher. Samuel turned to give chase, only to get tangled up with his own skates and fall. The winger was in alone. Pudge had covered his winger, and was too far away to cut him off. Simon came way out of his net — too far for Charlie's liking. A quick move and he wouldn't be able to get back. Which is exactly what happened.

The Tornadoes attacker faked inside, and then cut hard to his forehand. The move froze Simon. As a last resort, he threw out a poke check — and missed by a mile. That left a wide open net for a pathetically easy goal. Charlie would have laughed if it hadn't been against his own team. The game was only ten seconds old and the Hawks looked like novices.

"No worries, Mikey," Dunn said, clapping a few times. "Bad goal. The jitters are out. Get it back for us."

Mike promptly lost the draw again. This time he charged wildly after the puck. Zachary stayed back — smart thinking, as it turned out, because Mike went in too fast and missed the hit. The defenceman surged into the space vacated by Mike, gained the red line, and before Zachary could stop him fired the puck into the corner. Richard lumbered after it. The left winger beat him to it, and Richard tried another massive hit. This time only the boards felt it. He fell to the ice as the Tornadoes' forechecker gathered the puck.

Zachary and Pudge covered the pointmen. Mike was way out of position, hovering up near the blue line calling for the puck. The slot was totally exposed. The right winger saw he was uncovered, and raced to the open slot. His linemate fed him a sweet pass from the corner. Samuel dropped to his knees to block a shot that never came. The winger slipped it smartly to his centre, who one-timed it past a startled Simon.

Two goals in twenty seconds. Charlie wanted to get back on the bus.

"I think Sean was right about the score," Jonathon said in his ear, "except it'll be 10–0 for them."

"What's going on?" Charlie heard Mike yell on the ice. "This is garbage. You guys aren't doing anything," he said to Richard and Samuel.

Dunn kept Mike's line out. This time the Tornadoes centre pushed the puck through Mike's feet, slipping by to gather it up. Zachary anticipated Mike losing the draw and cut him off, flipping the puck back to Richard. He cut to the boards, expecting a return pass. Whether he was unnerved by the goals, or didn't understand what he was supposed to do, Richard ignored Zachary and tried to carry the puck himself. The Tornadoes centre stripped him of it in one motion, and would have been in all alone if Pudge hadn't stopped and hustled back. He lifted the player's stick, whirled around with the puck, and fired it the length of the ice. The whistle sounded for an icing. Head down, Zachary skated to the bench and called for a change. Charlie could see Zachary was angry. Sean's line filed out.

"Take it to them," Charlie encouraged. "Let's get one back, Hawks."

Mike was furious when he sat down.

"Worst shift I've ever seen. Is our D actually going to stop someone? Dad, I gotta get out there. This is sad. I'm going to have to kill someone before this game's over."

"Put it behind you," Dunn said. "Take a quick breather and get ready to go back out there." He looked over at Charlie. "Third line — move down the bench. You need to sit one off until we can get this game under control."

But there was no getting this game under control. The Tornadoes continued to dominate, the puck rarely leaving the Hawks' end. Charlie cringed over and over as he watched. Scott, Nick and the twins did their best on defence. Unless Zachary or Pudge was on the receiving end of their passes, however, the puck invariably bounced off a Hawks stick. Richard and Samuel were having a terrible time. The Tornadoes scorched the beleaguered pair for another two goals, one when a floater got behind them for a breakaway, and another after Samuel's foolish clearing pass from behind the Hawks' net ended up on a Tornadoes' stick and in the net. The score was 6–0 when the buzzer sounded to end the second period.

Charlie had never been benched in his life, and he suffered a thousand deaths watching as the Hawks were getting slaughtered. And apart from two short shifts in the second period, the third period began like the first two — with Charlie watching. The Hawks finally got some good news two minutes in. Zachary cut across the front of the Tornadoes' net to forecheck. A defenceman hooked Zachary with his stick and caught a piece of his arm. Zachary spun around and fell, and the referee's arm shot up for a penalty. Mike's line had been out since the start of the period, and Dunn had to change. Sean's line took over.

"Line one, thirty seconds and you're back out," Dunn bellowed. "Gotta get a goal already."

Jonathon elbowed Charlie. "If we ever get out again, why don't you take the faceoff?"

"I don't think Dunn would like that too much."

"I've always been a winger. Still don't know why you're not centering our line. I lost both draws I took today. Besides, what's he gonna do? Bench us? We've only been out for two shifts the whole game."

He had to laugh. Jonathon was right. Dunn couldn't exactly threaten them with less ice time.

A Tornadoes defenceman stripped Sean of the puck

and fired it down the ice. Dunn smashed his clipboard on top of the boards. It broke, and he threw it to the floor.

"Shaw, get me another clipboard," he ordered.

"Sorry, Mr. Dunn. We only have the one."

"Just great. What do you do here, anyway?" He waved his hand dismissively. "Mikey, take Sean's line off. They couldn't score a goal in twenty periods."

"Hold on a minute, Coach," Zachary said. He had his helmet off. "Something's wrong. I need to sit off another minute."

"Great!" Dunn yelled. "We need a goal and you're fiddling with your helmet. Fine, third line's up. Don't take more than thirty seconds." He cupped his hands to his mouth. "Sean, get off."

All three players on Sean's line skated over and Charlie and his linemates jumped over the boards. "Go for it, Charlie," he heard Pudge say.

Charlie's legs were tight as he skated to his end — not surprising, since he'd watched practically the entire game. Nick had the puck behind the net. He circled behind and took it, and Nick followed. A forechecker shifted across. Charlie put it into high gear and blew by him along the right boards.

"Take it in, Charlie," Nick yelled. "I'm with ya!"

Jonathon and David were on the wings up near centre. Charlie swerved to his left and continued up the middle. A second Tornadoes forward came at him. He slipped the disk to Jonathon, and jumped past. Jonathon gave it right back. Out of the corner of his eye Charlie could see Nick hustling up the left side. David had dropped back to cover.

The few Hawks supporters began to cheer — practically the first time in the game they had a reason. Charlie stormed into the Tornadoes' zone, the defencemen back-pedalling fiercely to prevent him from gaining the corner. Charlie stopped at the hash marks and the defender slid past. He then cut to the inside, parallel to the blue line. Nick continued on to the net, while Scott camped out in the slot, his stick raised for a slapshot. The defenceman panicked and charged at Charlie. He waited until the defenceman committed himself, then slid the puck between his feet to Scott. The defenceman covering Nick scrambled to intercept. Scott blocked him off with his body and passed to Nick. The goalie stacked his pads, thinking Nick would shoot. He was wrong. Charlie had slipped past the confused defenceman. Nick flipped a pass across the crease. Charlie had an open net for an easy goal.

Scott and Nick threw their hands in the air and pummelled Charlie on the helmet and back. "That felt good, dude," Scott said. "Taking candy from a baby or what?"

"Nice passing," Charlie said.

"Nice to have someone to pass to."

Jonathon and David joined the huddle.

"Awesome display, guys. That was beautiful to watch," Jonathon said.

Bang! Bang! Bang!

The noise caught Charlie's attention. He looked towards the bench. Mike was standing up, smashing his stick on the boards. He wasn't celebrating the goal, however.

"Joyce, change it up."

Charlie wanted to throw his stick across the ice. He scores a goal, and Dunn hauls him off the ice?

"I'm starting to understand our coach," Scott said. "The worse you play, the more you play."

"Hey, what's Zachary up to?" Nick said.

He was next to Dunn, his helmet still off.

Charlie skated over to the bench.

"Can I go on already, Dad?" he heard Mike plead.

Dunn was not paying attention. He'd gone down to the floor practically on all fours.

"What's up?" Charlie asked.

"A screw dropped out of my helmet," Zachary said. "We're looking for it. You guys stay out." He winked. It occurred to Charlie that perhaps the screw had not fallen out on its own.

Mike was in a rage. "Joyce, get off the ice!" he screamed.

"We gotta keep the lines together," Zachary said. "Take a pill, dude, and relax. Do you mind if I fix my helmet?"

The two boys faced each other. For a moment Charlie thought they were going to fight. Zachary stared right into Mike's eyes, even taking a step forward, their faces practically touching. That lasted a few seconds, and then Mike sat down, banging the shaft of his stick against the top of the boards.

"Totally bogus team," he muttered.

The ref's whistle blasted. "Line up, Hawks," he yelled.

Charlie raced to the circle. He barely had time to set up before the ref dropped the puck. Both centres missed it. Their sticks crashed together and the puck bounced to the side. Charlie reached out with his skate blade and kicked it back to Nick. He flipped it to David near the boards. The right winger took two steps over centre and fired it into the Tornadoes' zone. Jonathon was first in on the forecheck.

"Your puck, Jonathon," Charlie said, cruising in behind.

Jonathon impressed Charlie by first digging hard and winning the battle for the puck, and then skating away with it along the back wall. The Tornadoes centre left the slot to cut him off. The front of the net was wide open.

He raised his stick. "Quick pass," Charlie said.

Jonathon's head was down, though. He continued around the net for the wraparound. The goalie saw it coming and easily batted the puck into the corner. Charlie gave chase. A Tornadoes defenceman was there first and fired it around the boards and out of the zone. The puck slid deep into the Hawks' zone. Scott hustled back. Charlie saw Mike standing up at the bench.

"Joyce, change it up. Come on. Move it."

He ignored him. It was 8–1, and he'd hardly played all game. He wanted one more rush. He circled near his own blue line and Scott hit him with a hard pass. He had to swerve quickly to avoid a forechecker. The Tornadoes' centre pressured him next, but Charlie was able to swing past him with a neat move, slipping the puck between his skates. Nick joined the rush, with Jonathon on the left and David standing near the far blue line. Charlie headmanned it to Nick, and the smooth-skating defenceman hoofed it up the left side.

Nick crossed the blue line, holding up close to the

boards near the top of the circle, the right defenceman watching him closely. David went straight for the net, attracting the other defenceman. A Tornadoes forward charged Nick, bending down low, stick and right leg along the ice. That left a gap at the top of the slot. Nick saw it and saucered the puck over the forward's leg. Charlie arrived precisely as the puck touched the ice.

The goalie came well out in a deep crouch, glove hand up high. David and the defenceman battled for position in front. The goalie was playing him to shoot. Charlie was about to fake a shot and try a move short side, when he heard his name called. Jonathon was perched at the far side of the net, all alone. Charlie slid the puck across without hesitation.

"Lots of time," Charlie said.

Jonathon was either too excited or too nervous. Instead of stopping the puck and tapping it into the open net, he tried to deflect it in one motion. The puck slipped off the heel of his stick and into the corner. A Tornadoes player got the puck and iced it.

Tweet!

The icing call meant a line change. Disappointed, Charlie skated to his bench. A stick hit his shin pads.

"Beautiful pass," Jonathon said, shaking his head. "Could I have had more time? I thought there was a guy right on me."

Charlie didn't have the heart to tell him otherwise. Why bother? It would only make him feel bad about missing the open net. "It was a good play. You just fanned on it. Part of the game. You'll get the next one."

On the bench Jonathon smacked his linemates' helmets. "Not a bad effort," he said. "One goal, and we should have had another. Give us a bit more ice time and we'll tie this baby up."

Charlie knew that wasn't likely.

His line only got one more shift, and a short one at that. The Tornadoes answered Charlie's goal with three more of their own. The Hawks managed two late goals — both by Mike. His first came off a blistering shot from Pudge. The puck squirted between the goalie's pads. Mike had done little more than hang around the net all game waiting for Pudge and Zachary to feed him, and he was there to shovel the puck into the wide-open net. Then, with a minute left, Zachary went end to end before feeding Mike for an easy tap-in from three feet out. Mike celebrated each goal by pumping his arms and racing to the bench to slap gloves with the players on the bench.

"Goal scorer's goal!" Dunn declared jubilantly. "Did you see how he got himself into a position to score? Hey, Shaw, I told you he'd break free eventually." Coach Shaw smiled and gave a thumbs-up. "Two goals. I love it. But he can't win the game himself. I'm gonna need way more effort from the rest of you — and I'm gonna get it, trust me."

Jonathon elbowed Charlie's side. "A chair could have scored those goals," he said.

He laughed to be polite, although nothing seemed funny right now. The game had been a waste of time. All he'd done was sit and watch the Hawks be annihilated 10–4 by the worst team in the league. He corrected himself — by the second-worst team. The Hawks were most definitely the worst.

The Tornadoes players leapt over the boards to congratulate their goalie when the game ended. The Hawks skated slowly to their end. A few players slapped Simon's pads half-heartedly, and then the entire team followed Mike to shake hands. The Tornadoes goalie took Charlie's hand and held on.

"You're Charlie Joyce, right?" he said.

Charlie nodded.

"You hurt or something? Why didn't you play?"

He was at a loss for words. "Coach was trying new lines," he said.

The goalie looked confused. "I don't mind you on the bench," he said. "You made me look bad on that goal, and you almost got another on that pass across."

"You guys were too much for us today," Charlie said, letting go and moving down the line.

"What was the goalie saying to you?" Pudge asked, as they skated off.

"He played in the school tournament for Flemington. He remembered me."

"So what's your secret?" Zachary said from behind.

"Secret for what?" Charlie said.

"For getting off Mike's line. I didn't get a pass from him all game."

Zachary usually never let things bug him too much. He was obviously unhappy about the game. Who wouldn't be, after losing like that?

"I think we need to speak to the coach," Charlie said. "We three have to get on the same line. And I also have to speak to him about Matt. It'll be fine once we get the lines sorted out."

"I don't think he's the listening type," Zachary said.

"We'll have to make him listen," Charlie said, "or we'll lose every game we play."

9

EARLY BIRD

Charlie forced a spoonful of porridge into his mouth. He wasn't used to eating so early, and his stomach didn't seem to be awake yet. He added a third heaping spoonful of brown sugar.

"So, I'm hoping you're up at six-thirty in the morning to do some schoolwork," his mom said, joining him at the kitchen table. Charlie smiled awkwardly. School was a bit of a sore point between them. They'd had a few mother–son talks about him pulling his marks up. He wanted to, and he honestly liked school; he just never seemed to have enough time, especially with hockey. He also knew that his mom would never accept hockey as an excuse for not doing well at school.

"So . . . what exactly could motivate you to wake up at this hour? Have you decided to actually get to school on time?"

"Nothing so crazy. I have to meet someone before class and I don't want to miss him."

"Who are you meeting?"

"A guy."

"What guy?"

She wasn't going to like the answer.

"A guy from the hockey team. I want to go over a few things."

Her look hardened slightly. "Like what?"

Charlie hoped to patch things up with Mike. Pudge had told him that Dunn always dropped him off at school around eight o'clock on his way to work, which is why Charlie was up so early. Charlie figured the best way to get Matt on the team was to win Mike over, and then Mike could ask his dad. Charlie also wanted to talk to him about the lines.

"I want to ask him about some plays. I had an idea . . . and wanted his opinion."

His mom watched him closely, and Charlie had the uneasy feeling she was going to lecture him about school again.

"Try to eat a little more," she said. "You'll be starving in an hour. There are some bananas on the counter — they'll fill you up."

"Sure, Mom," he said, quietly relieved.

"I'm getting ready for work. I have to leave early too. Grandma's coming over to take care of Danielle until school. If you wait a bit I can give you a lift."

"Thanks, but I'll walk. I've got lots of time."

"Isn't it nice not to rush? Maybe you should get up this early every day."

"I think I'll stick to the old routine. Early mornings don't agree with me."

His mom ruffled his hair and kissed him on the cheek before heading upstairs.

He pushed the bowl of porridge aside. He couldn't do it. Maybe he could force down a banana. Besides, he was nervous about speaking to Mike. It was obvious

Mike wasn't his biggest fan. He'd have to think of something to say — and he had about thirty minutes to do it.

* * *

Charlie kicked a clump of dirt along the sidewalk as he made his way to school along the dark and empty streets. A voice startled him.

"Charlie, what's up?"

It was Dylan.

"How's it going?" he said.

"Not bad. What's got into you? School doesn't start for over an hour. You want to make sure you're on time for once?"

His lateness was becoming a school joke. He promised himself he'd start leaving earlier.

"Nah — don't want to mess with a good thing. I'm actually on my way to speak to your best friend about the hockey team."

"Best friend?"

"Mike Dunn."

Dylan laughed. "Sorry I can't join you. Band practice." He held up a large case.

"What do you play?"

"Bass guitar. Jazz band. Once a week we meet with Mr. Parker."

Charlie liked music. He'd taken piano lessons as a kid, but he'd never gotten into it. He'd rarely practised, and eventually his mom stopped the lessons.

"That's cool. I didn't know you played."

"You haven't heard me yet. Reserve your judgment."

"I'm sure you're good. That's just your modest

streak." He kicked the clump of dirt to Dylan, who passed it back. "How're the Tigers this year?" he said.

"Let's say average. We got thumped pretty bad by the Snow Birds — that's one awesome team. They've got J.C. Savard up front, Burnett on D, Alexi in goal, and the rest of them can play too. We did have a serious game against *your* best friend last night."

"Best friend?"

"Jake Wilkenson and the Wildcats."

This time Charlie laughed.

"Those guys are crazed," Dylan said. "Dirtiest team I ever played. Their coach is the worst. He tells his players to fight and spear — wait till you play them. We must have had three fights, and I think four guys from each team got kicked out."

Pudge had told Charlie all about the Wildcats' coach, Don Schultz. His teams invariably led the league in penalties. Some parents hated him, but others liked him because he produced winning teams.

"I guess Jake and Schultz were made for each other," Charlie said.

"Watch yourself when you play them," Dylan said.

"I'll be okay."

"I heard about your little encounter the other day — he's out to get you."

Charlie pretended indifference. "Not much I can do about that."

The school came into view.

"See you later," Dylan said. "I go around the back." He took a few steps and turned around. "And don't forget to say hi to Mike for me."

Charlie grinned and waved goodbye.

Interesting guy, he thought — always had something on the go. Charlie had major respect for anyone who could play an instrument. He took a seat on a bench near the parking lot. Mike came from that direction. He pulled out a book and began to read. He was so engrossed he didn't notice the time pass, and so was shocked to hear the warning bell. Mike still hadn't shown up. Just his luck! The one day he got up early Mike came late. What a waste of time.

He was about to give up when he saw Dunn's sports car speed past. Mike had barely closed the door before Dunn put it in reverse. He flew out of the parking lot and spun the car in the street to go forward, an impressive bit of driving that made the tires screech and attracted a lot of attention from the students gathered in front of the school. Charlie steeled himself and jogged over.

"Hey, Mike, you got a minute?" he said, in as pleasant a tone as he could muster.

Mike narrowed his eyes. "I guess. What do you want?"

"I want to talk to you about the team."

"Because . . . ?"

He wasn't going to make this easy. Keep your cool, Charlie told himself. "I wanted to ask what you thought about getting Matt Danko on the team."

"Team's been picked."

"I know. He missed the tryouts. His dad got laid off and he had to work after school. Anyway, Pudge was able to get him a job with more flexible hours."

"Yeah . . . and . . . ?"

"Okay. Well, he's got the time to play again, and

his dad's found lots of work. He's an amazing carpenter. He's building a ton of stuff for my mom's café, shelves and new counters, and I think he's lined up a few more contracts — at least that's what my mom told me."

"I can't tell you how overjoyed I am that he's building shelves for your mom. What's it got to do with me, or the Hawks?"

Charlie felt his temper rise. For Matt's sake, he took the abuse and continued calmly.

"Matt's a great player — you know that. He'd be a sweet addition to the team. We need more firepower up front. He's also a physical force, and let's face it, we're not the biggest team in the world."

"That's my dad's decision. I'm not the coach. Talk to him."

"I thought maybe you could talk to him. Get him on side."

"You thought wrong. We don't need Matt. Our problem is certain guys think they're better than everyone else."

Charlie flushed deeply. Mike was obviously referring to him.

"Let me give you some advice," Charlie said. "You're the captain, and the captain's supposed to bring the team together, not . . . not . . . make things up about guys."

"I'm not making anything up. I call 'em like I see 'em," Mike snarled. "Stop acting like you're such a superstar — and come off the ice when you're called!"

"That's spaced. I don't know what game you watched. I was on the bench practically the whole time.

While we're on the subject, if anyone needs to get off the ice it's you."

"Well, I scored, didn't I?"

"So what. I scored too."

"Aren't you just the superstar?"

"That's not the point. The point is . . ."

"The point is the other lines suck."

"And that's why we need Matt!"

"Forget Matt — and forget you. You're lucky to be on the team, Joyce. My dad already regrets picking you. Our team would be ten times better without a superstar wannabe like you . . . and get off the ice when you're called, Third Line Boy!"

He brushed past Charlie and marched towards the front doors. Charlie was so angry he felt like running after him. Then it occurred to him — and he allowed himself to smile. Mike hadn't said no; he'd told him to speak to his father. Well, Charlie Joyce would do just that.

The bell rang for the start of school. He picked up his knapsack and hurried to join the line. He had to laugh. Even when he got to school an hour early he was late.

10

THIRD STRIKE

Charlie caught up with Matt during the day. "What's Matt up to today?"

"I got a spare right now," Matt said. "Might head to the library and catch up on some work. I've been totally behind this term."

"I know that feeling," Charlie said. "I'll catch up with you after my class."

"Pudge told me you spoke to Mike this morning," Matt said in a low voice.

Charlie could see Matt was embarrassed. "I just wanted to talk about the team. I also asked about you playing, and he told me to speak to his father. I'm going over after school."

Matt groaned. "I gotta work."

"I know. Don't sweat it. I think he'll say yes, especially after the Tornadoes game. It was pathetic. We got totally smoked."

"Zachary filled me in. Said something about Mike playing the whole game."

"Things will sort themselves out. First thing is get you on the team."

Matt cleared his throat, rolling his neck slightly. "I'd

love to be out there — now that things have sort of gotten under control." He paused. "You don't have to do this, by the way. I mean . . . I should be the one asking. I could go later in the week."

"We can't wait another day. We need you out there like you wouldn't believe. It's going to be a long season as it is."

"Well, thanks. I appreciate it." He cleared his throat again. "And thanks for talking to Pudge and your mom."

Charlie cut him off. "Forget that. Your dad's doing my mom a favour. Just promise to set me up for a ton of cheap goals when you come out."

"I can do that."

Charlie looked at the clock on the wall. He was going to be late for his next class. He needed to say something first.

"It's no big deal," Charlie said softly. "I mean, about your dad and all. Things happen, and he'll be okay once he gets going. Don't let Jake bug you about it."

Matt's face turned red. "I guess. Not much I can say."

"That's not true. You don't have to take his dissing about your father — and if you want me to back you up, I'm there," he said fiercely.

Matt nodded and held out his fist, and Charlie punched it.

"See you later," Matt said, and he ran off down the hall.

The bell rang, announcing the start of the next period. Charlie groaned and ran down the stairs to get his science books, and then back upstairs, karate-kicking the hall doors open so he wouldn't have to slow down. He groaned again. Should have saved his energy. The door was closed. His life was one big late slip! He took a deep breath and went in. His teacher gave him a stern look, pointing at the clock. Charlie cast an apologetic look back and quickly took his seat. He caught sight of Scott off to the side, laughing. He suppressed a smile and opened his books. But try as he might, he couldn't stop thinking about meeting Dunn after school.

He'd already blown it with Mike. He couldn't mess up again.

* * *

Charlie crouched slightly on his skateboard, cruising down the hill towards Terrence Falls' downtown. The autumn air had a slight chill to it, although the cool air was welcome after a long day at school so he didn't mind.

Dunn's store was easy to find. An enormous orange sign dominated the street: *Dunn's Sportsmart — Play Hard . . . Live Large.* He'd been here once before. The place was amazing — equipment for practically every sport you could name: hockey, golf, tennis, skiing, soccer, lacrosse, running, cycling . . . Hard to imagine Dunn owned twenty more stores like this. He thought his mom's café was big. Fifty cafés could fit into this place.

He made his way to the cash.

"Excuse me. I'm looking for Mr. Dunn."

"In the back," the cashier replied.

"Charlie!"

Edward Shaw came over carrying an armload of hockey sticks. Charlie had grown to like his assistant coach. Charlie found he had a strange desire to help him out, even though he was an adult. He seemed sad most of the time. It couldn't be easy working for Dunn — and he didn't seem to enjoy coaching.

He told Shaw why he'd come. The assistant coach's eyes widened and Charlie saw a drop of perspiration run down the side of his head.

"I'm not sure that's the best idea. Mr. Dunn likes to do things his own way. He did say the team was picked."

"Matt's a great player, and he'd make a huge difference. He's great with the puck, and he'll also add some toughness."

Charlie saw that Shaw was uncomfortable with the idea, but he offered to escort him to Dunn's office anyway. They went to the back of the store and through a black metal door. Charlie felt like he was entering an alternate universe. The store was spectacular, so luxurious, clean and modern; the office area and warehouse looked more like a hockey arena. Concrete walls and floors gave it a depressing air. Boxes were piled up to the ceiling on rickety grey shelves and there was dirt everywhere he looked. A few men drove around in hydraulic lifts, moving large boxes around. Fluorescent lighting gave off a yellowish glow and a distinct buzzing noise. He couldn't imagine working in a worse place. He really felt sorry for Coach Shaw now.

Shaw pointed to a door to the right. In large, gold letters, a sign proclaimed: *The Boss Lives Here*. Charlie heard a loud voice from inside. Without warning, the door swung open and a man walked out, his face ashen, as if all the blood had left.

"Get here on time," Dunn's voice thundered, "and

make sure the shoes are unloaded from the trucks and stocked on the shelves before we open."

Dunn sat in front of a metal desk that ran the length of the room. Papers littered the desktop, with multi-coloured forms hanging from hooks in the wall.

Shaw cleared his throat. "Mr. Dunn, Charlie's here to see you, sir."

"Who?"

"Charlie Joyce, from the hockey team, sir."

"What does he want? We don't play until tomorrow."

"I know, Coach," Charlie said, stepping nervously into the office. Even in his sweatshirt he was cold and he had to force himself not to shiver.

The cold didn't seem to bother Dunn — he wore a short-sleeved shirt.

"I wanted to tell you about a good friend of mine, Matt Danko. Mike knows him. He played with the Wildcats last year, and the school team this year. He can play centre or wing. He scores, and hits too. He's a real all-round team player. I talked to Mike this morning, and he told me to speak to you."

Dunn's eyes narrowed.

Charlie's heart was racing. Deep down, he just wanted to run. But he wasn't going to let Matt or the team down. He forced himself to speak slowly. "He missed the tryout because of work, but now he's got a new job and can play. He'd really like to come out. I mean, maybe he could just come to a practice and you could see what he can do. Once you see him in action, I know you'll be impressed."

He had prepared an entire speech, but somehow he

couldn't remember the words. He mumbled about Matt being ready to come out any time, and then waited for Dunn to reply. Dunn nodded a few times. Charlie thought that was a good sign. Then he began to chuckle, at first quietly, and then louder and louder. Charlie's hopes began to fade. The laugh sounded nasty.

"I really appreciate you taking the time from your busy schedule to come down here and talk to me. As you can see, I don't have anything to do but discuss the Hawks. Isn't that right, Edward?"

Shaw smiled awkwardly, his face beet red. He looked as if he wanted to run out of the office.

"In fact, now that I think of it, I don't see why I even bother to coach. You know a lot more about hockey than me. Right, Joyce?"

"I didn't mean that," Charlie said.

Dunn interrupted. "It's not enough that I drop fifty grand on new equipment. It's not enough that I take time out of my incredibly busy schedule, running a chain of sporting goods stores, managing the distribution system, sales, marketing. That's obviously not enough for Charlie Joyce. You can do better, I guess."

Charlie remained rooted where he stood. He couldn't feel his legs.

"I'm glad you came, though," he said. "Now I can fix my mistake — something I should have done already. Instead of this Matt joining the Hawks, why don't you join him at that new job? You're too high maintenance, Joyce. I don't like your attitude. Never have, never will. I don't put up with problems. I take care of them, which is why I'm sitting here and you're going to get out of my store."

What? Charlie's mind was reeling.

"I was just . . ."

"Are you thick or something?" Dunn yelled. "You're off the team. It's over. So find the nearest exit and use it. And I want my equipment back in my store by seven o'clock tonight or I'll call the cops and have you charged with theft. Got it?"

Charlie stared uncomprehendingly at Dunn, who spun in his chair and began banging away on a keyboard.

A hand touched his shoulder

"Come with me, Charlie," Shaw said softly.

He followed him back into the store. Nothing seemed real. He felt like he was dreaming. Unfortunately, it was no dream.

"Don't worry about the equipment," Shaw said. "I can come by your house tonight after work and get it."

"I'm off the team?" Charlie asked.

"He doesn't take kindly to criticism. I had a bad feeling about your idea. Maybe I should have asked him."

"But I didn't criticize."

"I know," Shaw soothed. "He's been in a foul mood since the last game." He sighed and ran his fingers through his thinning hair. "I have a feeling he'll be in a foul mood most of the time now that you're gone. I don't know much about hockey, but from what I've seen you're the best guy we have."

"I can't believe it," Charlie said. He wasn't really listening.

"Don't worry about the equipment," Shaw repeated. "I'll get it tonight."

Charlie nodded. "Thanks, Coach Shaw. That would help out."

They shook hands.

"Edward, the boss wants to see you — now."

Another employee was motioning towards the back of the store.

"I have to get to work," Shaw said. He looked closely at Charlie. "You okay? You need a lift back? I could take my break early and drive you."

"Don't worry. I have my skateboard."

"I'll see you later — for the equipment."

He left the store. The guys were going to freak. He was the biggest loser ever. The dream team was over. Why couldn't he leave things alone?

He started back up the hill. Typical. No matter how hard he tried, things always got messed.

11

ALL FOR ONE

School wouldn't start for another hour, but Charlie was slowly heading over. He hadn't been able to sleep last night, and finally decided to eat and get out of the house. He'd managed to give his equipment to Coach Shaw without his mother finding out. That was silly; but somehow he couldn't stomach the idea of telling her just yet.

At least for once he was glad to get to school early. It would give him time to think about what he was going to tell the boys. They were going to be major-league angry with him. He'd totally blown it. First he convinced them to leave their teams, and then he managed to get himself kicked off the Hawks.

He turned the corner and couldn't believe what he saw. His friends were already there. Why'd they come so early? It didn't make sense.

Pudge spotted him as he crossed the street, and waved. Charlie waved back. May as well come out and tell them, he decided.

Pudge handed him a sheet of paper before he could say a word.

"Take a look at this," he said.

Coach Dunn,

The following players believe that Charlie Joyce has been unfairly removed from the team roster. We want him put back on the team, or we will all have to quit.

We only want what's best for the Hawks — we hope you do too.

Signed,

Pudge Moretti   Nick Katsopoulos   Scott Slatsky
Zachary Jackson   Robert Ryan   Christopher Ryan

"How'd you find out?" he said.

"Coach Shaw came to the restaurant last night, after he picked up the equipment from your house, and told my dad," Pudge said.

"I don't think Dunn will back down," Charlie said.

"He'd better," Zachary said.

"The whole thing's insane," Charlie said. "It's like a bad television show, except I'm actually in the show."

"And we're going to see this through," Pudge said.

"The way I see it, Charlie comes back, and he lets Matt on the team too, or he's seen the last of me — end of story," Scott said.

"I don't want you all to miss a season," Charlie said. "It's my fault. I shouldn't have gone to his store. Besides, you shouldn't suffer for my mistake." He slapped his thighs hard with his hands. "I'm sorry for all this. I messed things up."

"It's not your fault the guy's a jerk," Scott said.

"Maybe if I spoke to him again . . ."

"We talked it over," Nick said. "We're in this with

you, and we made our own decision to play with the Hawks. You don't have to apologize to me. That petition's going in, even if it only has my name on it."

"That goes double for me," Scott said.

Charlie felt honoured to have such loyal friends. "So what's the plan?" he asked.

"After school, we go to Dunn's store to hand over the petition," Pudge said. "Even the twins are coming to meet us."

"Do you think I should come?" Charlie said.

"We should probably do it ourselves," Pudge said.

"Makes sense," Charlie said. "I'll be at my mom's café."

"We'll come by after," Pudge said.

"And maybe have some pie . . . or a sandwich," Scott said.

"You guys having a practice and not telling me?" It was Jonathon. Julia was with him.

"How's it going?" Charlie said, adding, "Hi, Julia."

"The Hawks have had some interesting personnel changes," Scott said.

"Like?" Jonathon said.

"Like Dunn's kicked Charlie off the team for asking if Matt could join," Scott explained. "Can you believe it? We all signed a petition — Charlie's back or we walk." He called out to Pudge. "What about Jonathon? He could sign."

Charlie and Pudge traded an uncomfortable look.

"It's not fair to put him on the spot like that," Charlie said. "I think we have enough names."

"On the spot, nothing," Jonathon said. "Hand it over."

He took the petition and signed with a flourish. "If you guys leave, Mike'll never get off the ice."

They all laughed and began imagining what Dunn would say when they gave him the petition. Charlie and Pudge went off to the side.

"This is not the way to start a season," Charlie said.

"It's intense, but I don't see any other way."

"If anyone can pull this off, it's you. All I know is the guy hates me for some reason."

"Time will tell."

"This is all my fault. I'm such an idiot. I should've . . . I don't know . . . waited or something . . ."

"This isn't your fault," Pudge said. "Like Scott said, Dunn's the problem."

Charlie didn't respond. What could he say? This was going to be the longest day of his life.

* * *

All day Charlie kept imagining how Dunn would respond — and he was having trouble imagining him saying yes! Finally, after what seemed forever, the bell rang, signalling the end of school. It brought no relief, unfortunately, and he decided to go straight to the café and wait. It was fairly quiet when he arrived. A few people were having coffee and dessert.

"Hi, Mom," he said. "It seems slow today. What gives?"

She shrugged. "That's the café business. Busy when you don't expect it, and dead when you're ready for a horde. I probably don't need your help. You can go home and get ready for the game. Grandma's there with Danielle."

It was probably time to tell her. He steeled his nerve.

"About the game . . . I sort of had a bit of a run-in with Coach Dunn. I was asking if Matt Danko could come play on the team."

"I hear you mention my Matt," a man said appearing from behind a counter. "You must be the Charlie my Matt tells me so much about."

Even without being told, Charlie would have known instantly that he was Matt's father. Matt was just a smaller version. Both were stocky and broad-shouldered.

They shook hands, and Mr. Danko's enormous hand practically swallowed Charlie's. Now he knew where Matt got his strength.

"Hi, Mr. Danko. I forgot you were doing some work here. I like the new shelves. They look awesome."

"I use three different woods for shelf and panel and mix stain myself. Not too dark is key."

"Stanislaw has been wonderful," his mom said. "And he's already got five more jobs, but I'm not letting him go just yet."

"I stay until I finish," he said. He turned to Charlie. "Matt says you got him job at restaurant. Thank you."

"It was mostly another friend of ours — Pudge."

"I thank him too, then. Back to work now."

He ducked down behind the counter. Soon Charlie heard a light sanding noise.

"You were about to say something about your coach?" his mom said.

"Right. So I asked him if Matt could try out. I went to his store after school . . . to his office. All I did was ask about Matt and he totally lost it. Kicked me off the team. All I said was Matt would be a great addition. He accused me of trying to be the coach. The guy just hates me — and I've never done anything to him."

Before his mom replied he heard a familiar voice.

"Charlie, nice to see you again. Sorry about yesterday." Coach Shaw shook hands with Charlie and his mom. He seemed so genuinely glad to see him that Charlie had to greet him cheerfully.

"Nice to see you too. It wasn't your fault. Besides, you tried to warn me."

Shaw shook his head and whistled softly. "I don't understand that man. He has so much, and yet . . . Anyway, I got off work early today because of the game. I'll have the usual, Donna."

Charlie looked over at his mom. She winked at him and went off to the kitchen.

"I guess you've been here before," he said.

His former coach smiled. "I come here most nights for dinner — here or Bruno's Bistro. Like I said, I usually finish work later, except for hockey nights. I passed by yesterday after I picked up the equipment. Told your mother what happened. I can't tell you how bad I feel."

So his mom had known all along. "Excuse me for a second, Coach Shaw."

"Certainly, Charlie," he said, "and that's enough of the Coach Shaw. I prefer Edward."

Charlie laughed. "Okay, Edward. I just have to speak to my mom."

She was pouring a bowl of soup when he came into the kitchen.

"Sorry about not telling you last night," he said. "I guess I was in a state of shock. I hadn't even told the other guys on the team."

"Don't worry, honey. You had a lot on your mind. Edward was so upset. I almost felt worse for him than you. He's such a nice man, lives all alone since his wife died three years ago, and that . . . Sportsmart guy . . . treats him so badly. Edward comes in almost every night for a soup and sandwich." She cut two thick slices of bread. "Have you given any thought to playing for another team?"

"Not yet. I have to look around. Team rosters are kinda set. I'll probably have to play in a lower division, if at all . . ."

"We can talk about it later. If it makes you feel any better, Edward speaks very highly of you and your friends."

Charlie heard some loud voices. They were back! His nerves kicked in — he almost didn't want to know. He left the kitchen.

"Officer, arrest that man," Scott said, pointing at him.

He was laughing and all smiles. Charlie noticed that Pudge, Nick and Zachary were more serious. "What's the word?" he said.

"Go directly to jail, do not collect $200, and under no circumstances even think of playing for the Hawks again," Scott said.

Charlie's heart sank. "I figured he wouldn't back down. That settles it. I'll stay off the team — Dunn wins. You guys have to play. I'll feel ten times better if you do."

Pudge shook his head. "You don't understand. He kicked us off the team too. Took one look at the petition, crumpled it up, tossed it in the garbage, and told us to get out of his sight."

"Don't forget we have until four o'clock tomorrow to return his equipment or he'll call the cops," Zachary said.

"How many years in prison for being in possession of used shin pads?" Scott said.

"Minimum ten years," Nick said.

"I'll be like fifty years old when I finish high school," Scott said.

"You're being optimistic," Nick said.

"I'll have lots of time to study in my cell, though," Scott said.

Normally Charlie liked their kidding. Now it seemed forced.

"Can this get any worse?" he said to Pudge.

"Maybe that's the only good thing," he said. "Things can only get better."

Charlie pointed out Edward, and they all said hello. He seemed very embarrassed by the situation.

"You boys sit down," Charlie's mom said. "I'll fix you a snack. You look like you could use some nourishment."

"I could eat," Scott said.

"I know that," she laughed.

They tried to keep the conversation light-hearted and fun. Scott and Nick teased each other as mercilessly as ever. Charlie knew better. They were upset. No team — no hockey. He hoped Pudge was right. Things had to get better. He would give anything to make it up to his friends. But how?

12

A DOOR OPENS

Charlie sprinted up the stairs, pushed the doors open, and continued ahead at breakneck speed towards his homeroom. The class door was still open — he wasn't late yet! He charged into the room and ran right into his teacher. Charlie got the worst of it, bouncing off and staggering a few feet backwards. He reddened as he heard the other kids in the class laugh.

"I appreciate your desire to be punctual," Hilton said. "Perhaps if you arrived a little earlier you could walk into the room."

The entire class was laughing now.

"Sorry, Mr. Hilton," he said. "I guess I wasn't paying attention."

"An accurate assessment, Charlie," he said. "Do you think you can make it to your seat without throwing another bodycheck?"

His classmates giggled.

"I'll try."

He sat down at his desk and opened his notebook. The character sketch was due Friday. Most of that was done. A composition was due next week. He was in a bit of trouble on that front. He'd have to finish the rough copy over the weekend. At least hockey wouldn't get in the way.

"I want to speak briefly about the stories you're writing," Hilton said.

A crumpled piece of paper landed on top of Charlie's notebook. Pudge cleared his throat and nodded at it. Charlie opened it.

You hear about the Hawks' game last night?

They'd played the Wildcats — Jake's team. He shook his head. Another note followed.

Wildcats winning 14–0 by end of second. Had to leave — too ugly. Mike got new guys to play. Not sure if they'd ever played before!

Pudge scribbled a third note and tossed it over.

Shaw came to restaurant after game. Told me Dunn went ballistic — screaming, tossing sticks. He's pulling sponsorship. Hawks folded!

Charlie didn't know whether to laugh or cry. Dunn killing the Hawks — the perfect ending to a total disaster. He didn't have time to think about it, however. Hilton was in a questioning mood. He was going around the room asking every student about the story they were writing. Charlie's was about a mountain climbing expedition to Mount Everest. Five men reach the summit when a massive storm rolls in. The story was mostly about how they got down. Charlie's anxiety rose as Hilton came closer to him. The other kids would think the story was weird.

"Well, Charlie, what have you got?" Hilton said.

Charlie described the story, and read the opening paragraph.

"Sounds like a great idea," Hilton said, after he was done. "Pay attention to how you build the tension. Everything should be relaxed and fun until the storm hits, after which you need to pick up the pace. I'm looking forward to reading it. Good creativity."

A wave of relief rolled over Charlie. Praise from his teacher was hard to come by. He also noticed the class hadn't laughed or made fun of his idea. Maybe it wasn't such a dumb one after all.

Once he'd made the rounds, Hilton surprised them with a grammar quiz. He placed a sheet of paper, face down, on everyone's desk.

"You've got fifteen minutes. There are eight questions, so don't take too long on any one question. The test begins now."

Grammar was not Charlie's strongest subject, and he hated pop quizzes. He turned the test over nervously. Hilton had been drilling them on grammar for the past two weeks. At the end of the last class, Hilton had told them to review their grammar book. Charlie hadn't taken the advice seriously, and spent the night watching television to take his mind off the Hawks and his friends.

Charlie answered the questions as quickly as he could, but he was still shocked to hear Hilton announce the test was over. How could fifteen minutes pass so quickly? Seemed like two.

"That'll do it," he said. "Pens down and drop your tests on my desk on the way out."

Charlie hadn't finished the last question. Way to go, Joyce, he thought bitterly. Blew another test by being lazy. He was so irritated that he didn't notice Julia standing in front of his desk. Startled, he looked up at her.

"Hey, Julia. How'd you do on the test?"

She had probably done very well. Julia was a straight-A student.

She wrinkled her nose and shrugged.

"I think I did all right. Last question was kind of tricky. Don't know if I got that one." This was not exactly what Charlie wanted to hear. He'd barely had time to read it. "So Jonathon didn't tell me how things turned out with Dunn . . . with the petition."

"You wouldn't believe me if I told you," Charlie said.

"Try me."

"Dunn kicked everyone who signed the petition off the team."

Julia's eyes widened. "But that's, like, the whole team. Who's left to play?"

"You know Mike Dunn?" he said. "He managed to find some new players, and they got destroyed by the Wildcats last night. Mike's dad pulled his sponsorship. The team's dead."

"So who are you guys going to play for?"

Charlie's shoulders sagged. "That's the worst part. It was mostly my bright idea for the guys to switch to the Hawks, and it's probably way too late to get spots on another team — at any level. And it's all my fault."

"Can Mike's dad just kill the team like that?" Julia said.

"Why not?" Charlie said. "It's his team."

"I know he can stop sponsoring the team. But can he just take the team out of the league once the season starts? Isn't everything already paid for?"

Her words hit him like a bodycheck into the boards. It was insane, totally ridiculous, but he felt himself get excited just thinking about it.

"Dunn must have paid the league fee for the team," Charlie said. "I wonder if he can get a refund."

"I bet he can't," Julia said. "Not once the season's started."

"You might be right," he said. "Otherwise, teams could pull out halfway through and the league would be stuck with the cost of the ice time for the games."

Pudge came over. "How'd you do on the test?"

"Last question was tough," Julia said.

"I barely had time to finish it," Pudge said.

Charlie groaned inwardly. He pushed the test out of his mind. He had more important things to do. He needed to find out if Dunn had already paid for the Hawks — which might mean they could enter a team in its place!

"Excuse me, people," Hilton interrupted. "Please hand in your tests. I also believe you all have another class to get to."

Charlie dropped the test on his desk and headed off to science. His mind was whirling with plans. He'd have to act quickly. Find out if Dunn had paid all the fees, and then if the league would accept a new team. Every second he got more and more excited by the idea. The Hawks might be dead. But maybe the dream team was still alive.

13

CHARRED RICE

Charlie stepped out of the elevator. Taped to the wall in front of him was a small yellow poster. A hand-drawn green arrow pointed to the left, the words *East Metro Hockey League* written above it. The dinginess reminded Charlie of Dunn's office. Must be a sports thing, he thought.

A tiny woman with grey hair piled up into a bun and striking blue eyes, framed by the largest round glasses and thickest lenses Charlie had ever seen, sat behind a desk. She looked up from her computer.

"Hi. My name is Charlie Joyce. I spoke to you on the phone?"

"How can I help you?" she said.

He'd called her only an hour earlier. "I wanted to speak to the person who runs the EMHL . . . Steve Roberts?"

She brightened up. "Wonderful. I'll see if Stevie is in his office."

A moment later she was back.

"Come on in. Stevie will be right with you."

Charlie noticed the resemblance between Steve and the receptionist as soon as he walked in. He was extremely short and wore round glasses with thick lenses. He was on the phone, and motioned for Charlie to sit. Five minutes passed before he hung up. He spun his chair to face him and read something from a piece of paper. "So your name is Charred Rice?"

"Not exactly. It's Charlie Joyce."

Steve looked down at the paper, and shook his head. "Mother's hearing is not what it used to be. So you used to play for the Hawks?"

"That's right, sir."

"Can you believe what that Dunn fellow did? Gave me one massive headache, that's what! I've been on the phone all day trying to line up another sponsor. Do you think it's easy to replace a team once the season's started?" He stared hard at Charlie.

"No, sir . . . but I might have a solution."

"I'm all for that. First, can you shed any light on the situation? Why did Dunn pull out?"

"I don't really know."

He looked confused. "You told me on the phone that you were on the team."

"I was — and I don't exactly know why he pulled out. Could be the team got off to a slow start."

Steve shook his head and sighed deeply, slouching back in his chair.

"He loses a couple of games and quits. What a guy. He kept saying the Hawks would be a powerhouse — a new dynasty. Blast the Snow Birds out of the water, he said to me over and over. You sure there isn't another reason?"

"Sorry, sir," Charlie said. "I could ask around. Anyway, the reason I'm here, what I wanted to ask you

. . . well . . . I was wondering how much it would cost to keep the Hawks going. How much did Mr. Dunn pay?"

Steve scratched his head vigorously, and pushed his glasses back in place. "Depends on a lot of things. There's the equipment, sweaters, transportation costs, tournaments. Parents offset some of that, but the sponsor usually puts in a good chunk. Dunn said he was going first class, so I'm not sure how much he was going to pay. Then there's ice time for games and practices, plus insurance, not to mention registration . . . Adds up to quite a pile of cash, believe me."

"I was more interested in the registration fee," Charlie said. "What do the Hawks owe for that?"

He looked surprised. "Nothing, of course. Teams pay for registration, insurance, and ice time for games up front. Dunn paid all that — and it's non-refundable. He's been threatening me with lawyers and lawsuits. He can sue me, for all I care. He's not getting a penny back — leaving me a team short when the season's already started. Bad enough the Aeros cancelled. Now this. This league's gonna give me an ulcer."

He picked up the phone and pushed a button.

"Mom, can you bring me some mint tea? My stomach's all upset."

He hung up the phone. "I don't know what Dunn paid for practices. He probably put down a small deposit for the season. He'd lose that, for sure."

"So you're saying," Charlie cut in, "that the Hawks are all paid up for league fees . . . and I think you mentioned insurance."

"You got it. The only consolation is that it cost Dunn a ton of dough — makes up for the headache he's caused me. He thinks he's God's gift to hockey. Talked about building a powerhouse. Must have said that to me fifty times. Man, that guy's repetitive. He's like a broken record. Said the EMHL better shape up and be a professional organization or we'd be in trouble. Like we ain't professional!"

His mother came in and put a large mug on his desk.

"Can I get you a chocolate-chip cookie?" she asked Charlie.

"Thanks, but I'm not really that hungry," he said uncertainly.

"I'd love one, Mom," Steve said. "Do they have nuts?"

"No dear. I made those yesterday."

"I'll have a couple. You sure you don't want one, Charlie?"

He shook his head.

Once she left, Charlie leaned an elbow on the desk. "I think I have a team for you," he said earnestly. "I can take that headache away right now."

"Who's the sponsor?"

"I don't exactly have a sponsor. I'm working on that — very close actually. It's almost not a problem. More important is that I have the players. I can put out a competitive team. And, like you said, the registration fee, insurance, and ice time for games is already paid for."

Steve leaned forward, took his glasses off, and rubbed his eyes. He didn't speak until he had the glasses back in place.

"How old are you?"

"Fourteen."

He slumped back. "You can't run a team. The manager has to be at least eighteen, and you need a certified trainer at every game and practice."

"Not a problem," Charlie said. "I have an adult willing to run the team, and the trainer's all lined up. Our team will take the Hawks' place. You won't have to change your schedule at all."

Steve leaned forward again.

"And the team will be good," Charlie said. "Better than the Hawks. I promise."

"Good," Steve said. "Some people were saying the Hawks were barely an A team."

His mother came in with the cookies.

"What do you think, Mom?" he said. "Do you think this young man can put a team together?"

She squinted at him closely.

"I like him," she said. "He looks like a very nice boy. Do you enjoy school?"

"I like school very much . . . It's my favourite place . . . to go . . . to school," Charlie stammered.

"I think he's a very nice boy," she said.

"That settles it, then," Steve said. "I like you too. You have initiative. I'd rather have you in the league than that Dunn creep." He took a bite of his cookie. "Come here in the next day or two with your manager. We need to sign a contract and the insurance forms. You'll need a list of players, and they'll all have to sign a waiver. Are any of your players from the Hawks?"

"Most of the players will be," Charlie said. "A bunch of guys were playing, like me, but we stopped, or were told to stop, and now will start again, so I don't quite know . . ."

Steve stared at him.

"I'll bring the list tomorrow," Charlie said. "What time?"

"Any time after one o'clock."

"I'll be here," Charlie said.

"Charlie, you've taken a tremendous load off my mind. Made my day, in fact. By the way, when's the Hawks' next game?"

"Monday against the Hornets," Charlie said. "It's the start of the regular season. We'll be there."

"That's in only three days. You can really get it together for Monday?"

"Guaranteed," Charlie said.

"Amazing. I'm lovin' this. I'll call the Hornets' manager and tell him the game's back on. I'll see you soon."

He was just out the door when Steve called out, "Who's your coach?"

"We'll have all that information tomorrow," Charlie said.

He closed the door, his heart beating so fast he thought his chest would burst. It was incredible — the team was theirs for the taking. He began planning his next step on the way down in the elevator. His grandfather was the obvious choice to be the manager. As for a sponsor, a trainer and practice time, he was at a loss for the moment. But he'd work it out. He had to. But he would also need some help, and Pudge was his man — he knew Terrence Falls inside and out.

So the plan was coming together. He'd got the team. Next, he'd get Grandpa on side, and then Pudge. After that . . . well, he'd just have to hope and pray everything would work out.

14

BOMBS AWAY

Charlie pushed back up his driveway on his skateboard for what seemed like the hundredth time. Pudge was supposed to meet him at his house, but something must have happened because he was really late. Every second today was precious. This was a huge day for the new team, a make-or-break day, and he desperately needed Pudge's help.

As he glided back down the driveway, Pudge was making his way downhill on his longboard, weaving along the sidewalk to pick up speed. Charlie breathed a sigh of relief. He turned the corner and pushed hard to meet him.

Pudge slowed with a heel grind. "I probably would have made it to your house," he said with a grin, "considering I'm going down a hill."

"Way too stoked to wait the two seconds," Charlie replied. "I had a crazy idea yesterday, and now I could use your help. Sorry for bugging you on a Saturday morning, but it's kind of important."

Pudge held his arms out. "You got my attention. Sorry I didn't call back last night. We were out late for dinner. What's this crazy idea?"

"I was talking to . . . someone . . . and realized that Dunn probably had to pay all his league fees before the season started. I went to speak to the guy that runs the league — his name's Steve, or Stevie, which is what his mom calls him . . ." Charlie waved a hand in the air. "I'm losing it. His name's not important. What's important is he told me that the Hawks are all paid up, and he's not giving Dunn his money back."

Pudge's eyes got wider.

"So I told him that we would put a team together in the Hawks' place — and the guy said okay."

"How can we do that? We don't have a sponsor, a coach, a manager, a trainer — we don't even have a team."

Charlie kicked his skateboard up to his hand. "That's what I need you for. First off, you know this place better than I do. There must be a business or a store that would want to sponsor a local team. We don't need a big spender like Dunn. Sweaters and socks would be cool. As for a manager, the league said we only need an adult to sign the forms. My grandfather agreed to do it, and we'll do all the real work. We'll need a trainer, according to league rules, and that may be a problem, but I bet we can find one. Maybe Steve can help. As for a coach, that's taken care of."

"Who's the coach?"

"Us! We'll run the team. We know the game. We can do it ourselves. Let's put a team together and kick some butt on the ice . . . but we have to get it all done by Monday when we play the Hornets."

Pudge looked almost dazed. He folded his arms across his chest. "Joyce, you really are losing it. I knew you were crazy, but I didn't think you were this far gone." He winked. "When do we get started?"

Charlie let out a war cry and he and Pudge high-fived. "I knew I could count on you. I knew it. It'll be perfect. Trust me. It'll be totally cool to play together on the same team, and do things the way we want. Anyway, last night I counted about ten players to start with, which means the first rule is no one gets hurt."

Pudge was counting on his fingers. "I have you, me, Scott, Nick and Zachary. Where'd you get ten?"

"We might have to do some recruiting. I'm also counting on Matt, the twins, Jonathon, and Martin as goalie." He laughed. "As long as Mike Dunn's not on the team, who cares?"

"I like the sound of that."

"Here's the plan I came up with. I'm going to see the rink manager right now about practices. The guy who runs the league said Dunn may have rented all his practice time already and maybe we can use that. Could you call the guys and ask them to come to my house tonight? Don't tell them why. We'll spring it on them when we have everything worked out."

"I can do that. No problem."

"Awesome. Then we have to figure out something for sweaters and socks."

"I've got it!" Pudge yelled.

"Give it to me," Charlie yelled back.

"The Hockey Shop. The owner might help out. It's a store downtown. I think he sponsored my house league team when I was like seven or eight. We've been going there for years. Not upscale like Dunn's, but it's totally about hockey and the old guy that runs it is friends with my dad. It's worth a shot, anyway."

"Pudge, you're a genius. Let's meet back here in two hours, and we'll go over and beg for the team."

"Speaking of the team. We could use a name. Team doesn't quite cut it."

"I know. I've been racking my brain and nothing sounds right — the Terrence Falls Warriors, the Flyers, the Penguins . . . the Chiefs . . . the Ravens . . . the Pirates . . . the Mermaids . . . the Pathetic Team Without a Name. I can't think of anything."

"Let's not worry about it," Pudge said. "We'll figure something out."

"It's gotta be a name about us — the Shooters, the Titans, the Attack, the Blades, the . . . the . . ."

"Give it up, Joyce."

He grabbed Pudge by the shoulders. "I've got it!" he practically screamed. "The players will run the team, and we'll show Dunn how it's done, show the league for that matter. How about the Rebels?"

Finally, Pudge seemed as stoked as Charlie. "You deserve your own NHL franchise. It's awesome. I love it."

"Remember, you call the boys and I'll arrange the practice time. Meet back here and we'll go get a sponsor." He dropped his board to the ground and was about to race off to the rink when Pudge called his name.

"Do you really think we can do this? I mean, really do it?"

Charlie spun around. "We have no choice. We've got to. Otherwise, hockey's done this year, and that's not an option."

He waved and set off down the hill. He'd never been so excited about anything in his life. He felt as if he could fly to the rink, and as he gained speed he imagined that's what he was doing, soaring above the houses on his board. Any time the tiniest doubt crept into his head, he pushed it aside. This had to work. He'd let his friends down big time by getting them involved with the Hawks in the first place. It was up to him to fix it.

15

SIX O'CLOCK ROCK

Charlie picked up his board and went inside the arena. Next to the concession stand he spotted a sign — *Gus's Place*. The door was closed. Charlie knocked, and when Gus didn't answer he pushed it open gingerly.

The office was like nothing he'd ever seen. It was part snack bar, part registration centre, and part hockey museum. Equipment from past eras was stuffed into every nook and cranny — old skates under shelves, goalie pads piled up between filing cabinets, gloves hanging from hooks — along with an assortment of coffee cups, yellowed piles of paper, and forms impaled on a spike. A tornado could not have created a more chaotic scene.

Charlie spotted an old hockey stick leaning against a wall.

He flexed it a few times. It was incredibly stiff and heavy. The composite sticks Dunn had given them were like feathers compared to this.

"Easy does it with the stick, son. That's a collector's item."

Charlie whirled around. Gus stood in the doorway with a kind smile. "Signed by every member of the '67 Toronto Maple Leafs."

"Sorry," Charlie said. "I've never held a stick like this."

"Not too many around. Dave Keon gave me that. I knew him from junior hockey, back when he was not much older than you. Look, here's his signature."

Gus took the stick and started to read the names of the players — George Armstrong, Terry Sawchuk, Johnny Bower, Frank Mahovlich — all Hall-of-Famers.

"So what can I do for you?" he said.

"I play for, or played for . . . It doesn't matter, really. I was on the Terrence Falls Hawks, a bantam team. The sponsor pulled out and now . . ."

"I thought Dunn was sponsoring that team," Gus said.

"He folded the Hawks," Charlie said.

Gus spat into a nearby garbage can. "Nice of him to call and tell me. He rented a ton of ice. Don't surprise me none, come to think of it. Never liked that fellow. Don't much like his stores either."

"There's still going to be a team," Charlie said. "Some of the players have taken over — the team, that is."

"Who's coaching?"

"We don't exactly have a coach. We're going to coach ourselves. That's why we named the team the Rebels. My grandfather's going to be the manager. We wanted to talk to you about practice. We were wondering about the ice time Dunn rented? Is it already paid for?"

"Here's the thing," Gus said. "That Dunn fellow put down a deposit for the season — ten percent. Supposed to pay the rest every month. He took prime time too. Now I gotta fill that or the rink will lose money. Never did trust that fellow."

"Only ten percent," Charlie said. "How much would it cost for the rest?"

Gus reached under a pile of papers on his desk and pulled out a binder, flipping through the pages. He stabbed a page with his finger and held it up for him to see.

"Like I said, Dunn took prime time, either four-thirty or five o'clock on weekends and seven o'clock on weekdays. Since he took so much ice, I gave him a deal — two hundred dollars an hour. There's cheaper, of course, but you guys got school, so it don't help you none."

"That might be a bit expensive for us," Charlie said.

He did his best to hide his disappointment. They'd never be able to afford that, not even with Dunn's deposit. Maybe they were fooling themselves about the whole thing. They had to practice.

"There is another possibility," Gus said. He stroked his chin slowly. "I want to help you out. I admire your spirit. How does free ice sound?"

"Sounds awesome," Charlie said.

"We only rent the ice starting at seven in the morning. Before that we're empty, but I'm always here early. You could practise from six to seven, before school or on the weekends before house league starts, and I'll just run the Zamboni over it. Dunn's deposit will cover the cost."

Charlie smiled weakly. Six o'clock in the morning! The guys wouldn't be too stoked about that. "That's very nice of you to offer," he said. "Are you sure there's nothing else?"

"Nope. We're booked solid. Only other thing is the prime time ice Dunn rented."

No real choice, he considered. It might even help him get to school on time. "We accept the offer," he said, extending his hand.

Gus took it. Charlie underestimated the man's strength. He looked to be over seventy years old, but Charlie had to force himself not to wince as Gus squeezed tight. Gus took no notice and continued with the bone-crusher. He then reached into a desk drawer, removed two elbow pads, a magic marker, a box of elastics and three Styrofoam cups, and pulled out a form.

"Fill this out — I need your contact information. Use any dressing room you want. Only one rule — off the ice before seven so I can run the Zamboni."

"That's awesome, Gus," Charlie said. "We'll let you know in a couple of days when we'll start."

"Good luck to you," he said.

Charlie had mixed feelings as he headed back home to meet Pudge. Six o'clock in the morning — killer! He could barely get to school on time, and that started at nine. On the other hand, thanks to Dunn, it was free ice, which was another lucky break. If it meant playing hockey this year he'd just have to suck it up and do it. He just hoped the rest of the guys felt the same way.

* * *

Charlie followed Pudge as they sped along the main street on their boards. They rode past Dunn's and turned left onto a small side street. After a few blocks, Charlie saw a bright red sign — *The Hockey Shop*. A mannequin with goalie equipment and a Detroit Red

Wings sweater stood in the window, framed by two large stacks of skate boxes.

"This whole place could fit into the stick section at Dunn's," Charlie said.

"I know, but it's a classic, old-time hockey store. No clothing or yoga stuff — just hockey. You'll love it. I never go to Dunn's. This place is totally cool. The owner's name is Mr. Sanderson, and like I said he's getting a bit old, so speak loud or he won't hear you."

Charlie understood why Pudge liked it so much the second he went in. Every square inch was crammed with equipment. Not necessarily the most expensive or trendiest stuff, but good quality. He saw a sign: *The Used Equipment Paradise*. He went over.

"Hey, Pudge. Check out these gloves. Mint condition and only twenty-five bucks. I think he just re-palmed them."

"He always has good deals," Pudge said.

Charlie needed a new pair now that Dunn had taken his equipment back. His old ones were falling apart. He put them on and flexed his fingers. "Perfect," he murmured.

"Gentlemen, what can I do for you?"

A man smiled at Charlie from behind a row of sticks. Charlie didn't think he looked very old.

"Can we speak to the owner?" Pudge said.

"You're looking at him."

Charlie could have cried. A new owner! He wouldn't know Pudge. Now what would they do?

"Is there another owner . . . someone's who is not . . . so . . . tall?" Pudge asked.

"Are you referring to a silver-haired man, perhaps?

That's my dad. He's finally retired. I've taken over. My dad was eighty-two years old and he still wanted to work every day. I finally convinced him to relax. He's taking his first holiday in thirty years, maybe more. He's off to Florida — I sent him."

"I've been coming here forever," Pudge said. "And this is my friend, Charlie — his first visit."

"An old customer and a new one — good combo. Let's make it official." He walked around and shook their hands. "Name's Brent Sanderson."

"Nice store you got, Mr. Sanderson," Charlie said.

"Mr. Sanderson's my father. Call me Brent, or you'll have to leave." He laughed heartily. "Thanks for the kind words, Charlie, but I know this place is a dump." He silenced their protests with a wave. "Just compare this to Dunn's Sportsmart. He gets fifty customers to my one. I've been after my dad to modernize for years. We'll always focus on hockey. But we need to expand, be better organized, and display the merchandise more professionally. Who can find anything in here? And I gotta change the name. In the future I want to sell more than just hockey equipment."

"I'll miss this store when it changes," Pudge said.

"I will too," Brent said. "Everything has to change at some point, though. So, can I help you find something?"

"We're in a slightly weird situation," Charlie said. "Our hockey team folded a few days ago."

"What happened?"

"The sponsor pulled out."

"That's not that bantam team — the one Dunn is sponsoring?"

Charlie nodded.

He looked at him intently. "Are you Charlie Joyce?"

He nodded again.

Brent clapped his hands. "One of my cousins knows you — Dylan."

"I live down the street from him."

"I was just over there for dinner last night. Small world or what?"

"Dylan's a good guy," Charlie said. "Good player too. Plays for the Tigers."

"He told me about the Hawks; and I know all about Dunn."

Charlie and Pudge exchanged glances.

"That's sort of why we're here. We're putting together a new team. We have a game in two days and don't have sweaters or socks," Charlie explained.

"What's the budget?" Brent said.

Charlie dreaded that question. "Not good, I'm afraid. We were hoping for something in the bargain-basement range."

Brent put his hands on the end of a stick and rested his chin on top. "I'll tell you what. I'll provide the sweaters and socks, as long as I can put the store's name on the back. I can't afford to sponsor the team like Dunn, but I can do that much."

Charlie couldn't believe his luck. Free practice time and now free sweaters! The Rebels were on a roll.

"When did you say you needed them?" Brent asked.

"Monday night."

"That's pushing it, but I have a few contacts that might help. Worst-case scenario, I have some practice jerseys, and can have the real ones ready for the next game."

"Awesome. I don't know what to say," Charlie said. "What's the team name?"

"The Rebels," Charlie and Pudge proclaimed together.

He nodded approvingly. "Good name. I like it. If you'll excuse me, gentlemen, I need to make some calls. Leave everything to me."

The boys thanked him and left. Only when he got outside did Charlie realize he was still wearing the hockey gloves. With a cockeyed grin he held them up.

"Nice move — steal from the sponsor," Pudge said.

"Next time I should try on a pair of skates," Charlie joked.

He went back in. Brent was sorting some paperwork.

"Brent, I wanted to ask you about these gloves. I forgot I had them on and walked out." He waved his hand.

"On the house, Charlie. Enjoy."

"Are you sure?" he said uncertainly.

"No worries."

"Thanks a lot. And thanks again for the sponsorship."

"Happy to do it," he said, turning back to his paperwork.

"You won't believe it," he said to Pudge when he got outside. "He gave them to me."

Pudge looked at the gloves. "Next time, remind me to put on some hockey pants. I gave mine away because of Dunn's equipment. The only pair I got is like two sizes too small. They fit like cycling shorts."

Charlie dropped his board to the ground. "Now

that I have my racing gloves, the first one to my mom's café is the winner."

He pushed off and tore down the street.

16

REBEL YELL

Pudge had organized all the guys to come to Charlie's house at five o'clock. Charlie and his grandfather were waiting in the dining room for them to arrive. He'd asked his grandfather about being the manager after his meeting with Steve Roberts. Even though he barely knew anything about hockey, he agreed immediately.

The problem of finding a trainer was solved almost as easily. Shirley, his mom's assistant manager and pastry chef, had been by on Friday night, and burst out laughing when she heard what he needed.

"Talk to my son, Jeffrey. He's in his first year of college in physiotherapy, and needs some practical training hours. He's been looking for something. I'll call him right now."

A minute later, Charlie had lined up a trainer!

After the crazy few days he'd had, he could barely contain his excitement to tell the boys about the new team.

"Can you come into the kitchen?" his mom called. She pointed to two large trays filled with sandwiches and cookies. "You can carry these downstairs. I have to run to the café for half an hour. Do you need anything else?"

"No, we're cool — and you didn't have to do that."

"Yes I did. Now have fun, good luck, and I'll see you soon."

Charlie ran the food downstairs. As he came back up he heard a loud noise outside, followed by cheering. He went to check it out. Zachary was lying on the ground at the bottom of the steps, his skateboard off to the side. One shoe was off.

"Try again," Scott said. "I'm sure you'll nail it this time."

"What happened?" Charlie said.

"Zachary rode his board down the steps," Nick said.

Zachary sat up, reaching for the board. "I almost made it, too," he said.

"You almost broke your neck," Pudge said.

Zachary got up, holding the errant shoe. He brushed off his pants, which were ripped at the knee. "My shoe got dirty, dudes," he said, pretending to be angry. "What am I supposed to do now?"

"I'd try again," Scott said.

"That's exactly what I was thinking," Zachary said.

"How about you do that later?" Charlie said. Zachary was the type who *would* try again. "My mom put out some grub downstairs. Go get some nourishment. Pudge and I have some big news and you'll want to hear it on a full stomach, especially Scott."

"What are you up to already?" Nick demanded.

"The rest of the guys will be here soon and all will be revealed," Charlie replied. "Now, be good little boys and head on in."

"Are you sure we don't have time to see Zachary wipe out again?" Scott asked.

"Maybe after," Charlie said.

"How about we just throw him down the stairs?" Scott offered.

A well-aimed shoe hit Scott in the chest.

"A hostage," Scott declared, grabbing the shoe. "To the toilet with you."

He opened the door and bounded down the hall, yelling, "Attack! Attack!" Zachary gave chase, with Nick close behind. Charlie had half a mind to join in the fun, but decided he should wait outside for the others.

His grandfather poked his head out.

"Based on the herd of elephants that just charged downstairs, I assume the team has arrived."

"Some of them, Grandpa," Charlie said. "The rest should be here soon."

"I'll be upstairs if you need me. By the way, what's with the shoe? One of your friends was punching it," he said. The corners of his eyes wrinkled, and he chuckled.

Only Scott could take it to that level, Charlie thought. Robert and Christopher came next, arriving together as always. He and Pudge went down the steps to greet them.

"How's the defence pair doing?" Charlie said. Charlie knew how quiet they were, so he wasn't insulted when they merely nodded in reply. "Thanks for coming over. Some of the guys are already here, so head on downstairs. There's lots of food. My mom's a cook and it's good stuff."

"Pudge said you have some info about hockey. What's up?" Robert asked.

"We'll fill you in once everyone gets here," Pudge replied.

Jonathon and Martin arrived.

"Couple more guys and we got ourselves a road hockey game," Jonathon said.

"Sounds good to me," Charlie said. "Greatest game on earth."

"I'd love to pound a few tennis balls past Martin," Jonathon said.

"No chance," Martin said. "I play out in road hockey. I'm a goal scoring machine off the ice."

"I love playing net," Charlie said. "We'll switch positions."

"I thought we were here for ice hockey," Robert said, uncertain if they were serious.

"Did I hear you say road hockey? I'll get my stick."

"Dylan! Are you coming to join our little meeting?" Charlie said. "Or is this just a tease?"

Dylan feigned indifference. "I didn't have much to do tonight. Pudge called me today and, since I was out for a walk anyway — well, I thought I'd come over and check things out."

He winked and followed the twins, Jonathon and Martin inside.

"Looks like everyone's here, except for Matt," Charlie said to Pudge. "Let's do this thing."

Zachary and Scott were engaged in an intense air-hockey game — last year's Christmas present from his grandparents.

"Sorry to bother you guys," Charlie said. "You can get back to your homework later."

"I gotta teach Zachary some respect for his elders," Scott said.

"I'm older than you," Zachary said.

"I'll just teach you some respect then."

They stopped their game and sat down. This was Charlie's favourite room. It had two large couches and he could just hang out and watch TV or play video games.

"First off, I want to thank everyone for coming," Charlie said.

"Sounds like a marriage speech," Scott said.

"Couldn't be. Julia's not here," Nick said.

Charlie ignored them. He continued in a serious tone. "We all had different reasons for joining the Hawks. Some wanted the challenge of triple-A, some were just looking for a team, and some didn't want to play for the Hawks at all." He pointed accusingly at Dylan, who bowed back.

"Pudge and I had an idea, and we wanted to get your opinion."

"It was Charlie's idea," Pudge piped in.

"Maybe at first, but Pudge helped to make it happen."

"What happened, already? What's the deal?" Nick cried.

"The Hawks are dead — Long live the Rebels!" Charlie declared.

The guys stared at him.

"I guess I should start at the beginning. I spoke to the guy who runs the league. We can take over the Hawks and put our own team in. Dunn paid for the league registration. We have a sponsor — the Hockey Shop; a name — the Rebels; a manager, a trainer . . ."

"We've got your mom's cookies," Scott said, holding one up.

"True," Charlie agreed, laughing along with the others. "And since we've all played tons of hockey, I figure we also have a coach — us! We can coach ourselves."

There was silence for a few moments.

Then absolute mayhem broke out. Soon they were all chanting, "Re-bels! Re-bels! Re-bels!"

Scott held his arms over his head to quiet things down. "I got a question," he repeated a few times. "Be quiet, you animals." He lowered his arms. "We do need one more thing — a captain."

"I nominate Charlie," Pudge said.

"I second it," Scott said.

"I third it," Nick followed.

"I fourth it," Scott said.

"You already seconded it," Nick chastised. "Now we have to do it again."

"Come on, guys," Charlie said. "We should do this properly. I'll hand out ballots and we can nominate a few people."

"I think you're captain," Christopher said.

That surprised Charlie. Christopher rarely said anything, especially in a crowd. Charlie looked around the room. His eyes met Pudge's.

"Move on, captain," Pudge said.

He didn't respond for a few seconds, a bit overwhelmed. "Thanks, guys. I appreciate it," he said finally. "Now stop interrupting me, Scott, and let me finish for once."

"The guy's captain for less than a second and he turns into a dictator," Scott said.

"We got lucky with uniforms," Charlie said. "The

owner of The Hockey Store is giving us sweaters and socks for free."

The guys all cheered.

"Before you get too stoked, wait till you hear about practices. Sir Thomas Dunn, our former sponsor, put down a small deposit at the Ice Palace. But that's for prime time and we can't afford that. So I spoke to Gus Wilson, the rink manager, and he'll let us practise in the morning for free, thanks to Dunn's deposit. We just have to promise to be off the ice before the next group so he can run the Zamboni."

"What time are we talking?" Zachary asked.

"Believe me when I say that this will hurt me as much as it hurts you . . . We can practise at six o'clock in the morning — that's 6 a.m."

"Ouch," Scott said. "Mega-ouch."

"It's a killer," Charlie said, "but it's all we can get. We'll only practise one or two times a week to keep the pain to a minimum. We need to commit to it, though. We have to practise, or this whole thing will be a waste. We can't just play games and expect to compete."

He looked around the room again. "Is everyone still in?"

They all nodded or flashed a thumbs-up.

"We're also short a few bodies. Right now, we have four defencemen and six forwards, which is okay but it's an injury away from being seriously undermanned. As it is, most teams will have an extra line and another pair of defencemen — we're going to have to really be in shape or teams will wear us down by the third period."

Matt walked in. "Did you count me in that number?" Charlie held out his first and Matt gave it a punch.

"You ever played hockey before?" Scott said.

"Don't tell me *you're* on the team," Matt said.

"I'm probably the best player."

"Then I've played before."

They laughed, and Matt flopped down on the floor.

Charlie hadn't seen Matt in such good spirits in a long time. He hoped it meant things were better at home.

"Don't get too excited, Matt," Zachary said. "We practise at six in the morning."

"That's great," Matt said. "It won't interfere with school or work."

"This guy's too upbeat for me," Scott said. "I say we kill him."

Scott leapt onto Matt, and they started to wrestle.

Everyone had a good laugh as Scott and Matt pretended to knock each other around, WWE-style.

"One last thing," Charlie said when it was over. He could tell the guys were restless. "The game against the Hornets on Monday starts at seven o'clock at the Ice Palace. Let's show up an hour early. We all need to sign medical release forms, organize sweaters, and handle a few other administrative details. That about covers it — no need to clear out, by the way. Feel free to hang out."

Scott jumped up on the couch. "I need to apologize to all of you in advance," he said. "I am about to crush each and every one of you at air hockey. No tears, please. Simply accept that I am the greatest player to ever hold an air hockey paddle."

He hopped over the back of the couch and grabbed a paddle, holding it to his heart. Nick took the other paddle, and held it to his.

"I feel a tournament coming on," Nick said. "First to three wins. Champion plays on. Last man standing is declared champion of all time."

Scott nudged Charlie with his paddle. "You should warm up. You'll be playing me in two minutes, after I destroy this pathetic air-hockey impostor."

They all crowded around the table, trading jokes and laughing at Scott's antics. Charlie noticed Matt standing off to the side near the couch. He wandered over to him.

"How's it going?" Charlie said.

"I'm beat. The restaurant is crazy on Saturdays. I was running from the second I got there. Pudge makes it look easy. I'm always on the brink of disaster."

"You'll get the hang of it," he said. "Anyway, good to see you back."

"I missed it more than I thought. I'm lucky to be working for Pudge's dad. He's given me flexible hours, so I can make all the games." He lowered his voice. "Thanks for helping my dad out . . . I . . . um . . . appreciate the help . . . and for taking on Jake and those jerks, and . . ."

"I didn't do anything," Charlie said. "Just mentioned that your dad was available. You should see the work he did at the café — amazing. As for Jake," he shrugged, "I somehow doubt that'll be the last time we tangle with his crew."

Scott let loose a huge scream. "How is this possible?" he wailed.

He tossed his paddle to Charlie, his head lowered. "Gentlemen, we all know Nick's a cheater. That's the main thing. Now excuse me while I have a good long cry."

Charlie faced Nick across the table. "Nick, I'm afraid your championship run is about to end. Maybe it's best if you just quit now and spare yourself the humiliation."

Nick rapped the disk at his net in reply. Charlie blocked it, and the game was on, with most of the onlookers calling next game.

17

BRING IT ON

Charlie tugged on his grandfather's sleeve.

"What time is it?" he asked.

"The game starts in thirty minutes."

He had to force himself not to try to rip the armrest off the van door. "I told everyone to be an hour early."

"Perhaps we should have left to pick up the sweaters and socks a bit earlier," his grandfather said quietly.

He was right. Charlie had wanted to see the end of a TV show, which would have been fine if they hadn't hit a ton of traffic on the way to The Hockey Shop. He was feeling sick to his stomach.

"Why don't I let you off in front?" his grandfather suggested. "Take your equipment in and I'll bring the rest of the stuff."

"It's okay. I can handle it. Just drop me off."

They pulled up in front of the arena.

Charlie was out of the car in a flash. He slung his hockey bag over one shoulder and the bag with the sweaters and socks over the other. With sticks in hand, he staggered towards the doors.

"You sure you don't want some help?" his grandfather called from the car.

"I'm good. See you in the dressing room."

He felt a surge of pride when he saw *REBELS — Room 6* written in chalk on a board in the lobby. The past five days had been a blur, a real whirlwind adventure. What had started during that road hockey game at his house was now a reality — he was playing hockey with all his friends, and this time without Mike or his dad to ruin it.

He pushed the door open.

"What's in the bag, captain?" Scott asked. "Presents?"

"Only good boys get presents," he said. "You've been naughty lately."

"I think I ate a carrot yesterday — that's a serving of vegetables."

"That was a cheesie," Nick said.

"At least it was orange," Scott said. "Close enough."

"The sweaters are in the house!" Charlie announced. "Sorry I'm late. Got stuck in traffic."

"What do they look like?" Pudge asked.

"Don't know. We didn't have time to see."

Charlie opened the bag and pulled one out. He stared at it in horror. The logo was beyond ugly. An ogre wearing hockey equipment, his eyes shut tight, was winding up to take a slapshot, all against the background of a purple puck. *REBELS* was spelled out in bold green letters below the logo and on the ogre's sweater. The colour of the sweater was even worse. The store name on the back was about the only thing he could handle. Charlie braced himself for everyone's reaction.

Pudge grimaced as if he'd eaten something bitter. "Is that pink?"

"Closer to light red," Charlie suggested, but he wasn't so sure.

"I'd rather not wear a sweater," Zachary put in.

"I tend to wash out in pastels," Scott said.

Nick nodded. "Maybe garbage bags would look better."

The avalanche of insults that followed was difficult for Charlie to handle. He wasn't crazy about the colour either, but no one seemed to appreciate Brent's generosity, or his hard work in getting the sweaters ready for the game. And speaking of the game, it was starting soon and they had more important things to deal with.

He handed out the sweaters, gritting his teeth as the sarcasm continued. His grandfather came to his rescue. He opened the door and, pointing to his watch, said, "Boys, I think you should all finish getting ready for the game. The Zamboni is just going on."

"We can complain about this later," Charlie told the others. "I gotta get dressed. Then we'll do lines." He raced to an open spot and hurriedly began to put on his equipment. As he was tying his skates he heard a few of the guys laughing.

"It's a nice look, Joyce," Scott said.

Charlie shot him a puzzled glance. Scott pointed at his legs. Charlie felt like punching the wall. He'd been in such a rush he had tied his skates before putting on his hockey pants.

He and Pudge had worked out the lines that morning, so at least that was ready. "Defence is set," he announced. "Scott and Nick, and Christopher and Robert."

"Do I have to play with him?" Scott said. "He can

barely skate." He threw a glove at Nick, who caught it deftly and threw it back in one motion. Scott raised his arm to toss it again.

"Cut it out, guys," Charlie barked. "No fooling around right now, okay?"

Scott raised his eyebrows in surprise. Nick shrugged and looked down at the floor. Charlie felt bad yelling at his friends; but someone needed to organize the team, and if he didn't, who would?

"Matt and I will take centre. Zachary and Dylan go with Matt, and Pudge and Jonathon will play with me. Quick changes today, guys. We only have two lines and we'll get tired. Thirty second shifts and come off. Defence, you're on your own. Change when you like. We'll deal with penalties when they happen."

Bang. Bang. Bang.

The referee opened the door.

"You guys playing? The game's about to start."

Charlie's head was spinning. He'd lost track of time. He needed a watch. "Let's get going, boys." They all looked at him.

"Captain should lead us out," Pudge said.

Charlie noticed that every player was looking at him. He'd been behind this team from the start, and they would take their cues from him. Time to show some leadership.

"We'll be out in a second, ref," he said, and the door closed.

He stood up. "If anyone needs some motivation, just picture Dunn's face when he hears we won our first game. Maximum effort, play smart, no penalties, and we'll handle the Hornets easy. This is our team. We win together and we lose together. I'd rather do the first!"

He wondered how they'd react to his pep talk — especially Scott and Nick, after he'd just yelled at them.

"Charlie's right, boys," Scott said. "We play as a team and no one can touch us."

"These guys ain't nothing," Nick growled.

"Full speed," Zachary said. "Game should be over after the first period."

As usual, his friends were proving to be team players. He took a deep breath. Joyce, you'd better play the game of your life, he said to himself.

"Let's do this," he said, and led them out the door. They began chanting, "Re-bels! Re-bels! Re-bels!"

He fairly leapt through the door, his blades cutting deeply into the gleaming ice. He circled their end as fast as he could, trying to calm his nerves as much as anything. After a few laps he grabbed a puck and began peppering Martin with shots from in close, rifling a dozen wrist shots into Martin's pads to let him get a feel for the puck and then working his glove hand. Once he saw Martin was ready, he backed up to the blue line and, joined by the rest of the team, fired slapshots from the point.

Bhrrr!

The horn blared to signal the end of the warm up. Charlie peeled off for a final lap around the net. A cowbell rang out.

"Yeah, Charlie! Go, Charlie, go!"

It was Danielle. Charlie waved to her. His mom and grandmother were there too, and they waved back. He coasted to the bench.

"Who's starting?" Zachary asked.

He felt stupid. How could he have forgotten to announce that?

"Matt's line," Charlie said, as if he'd known all the time. "Scott and Nick on D."

He figured it would be too much to start himself. He sat down on the bench, flanked by Pudge and Jonathon, and looked over at the Hornets bench. It was packed.

"They have three lines," he told Pudge.

"We need to keep the shifts short," Pudge said.

Charlie's grandfather tapped him on the shoulder pads. Jeffrey stood beside him.

"Do you need us for anything?" he asked.

"Grandpa, could you handle the door for the forwards?" Charlie said. "Jeffrey, can you take care of the defencemen?"

"Will do," Jeffrey said.

The referee held up his hand to each goalie, and they signalled back that they were ready. He held the puck aloft for a second, and then dropped it. The game was on. Matt batted it forward and gave chase. The right defenceman tried to carry it outside to the left, but Matt was too quick. He lowered his shoulder and bowled him over.

Charlie pounded the boards with his stick, leaping to his feet. "Awesome hit, Matt," he yelled.

Zachary swept in from the right wing to scoop up the puck, and headed towards the Hornets' goal. The left defender shifted across to force him outside. As soon as he committed himself, Zachary flipped the puck softly across the blue line and crashed into him. Both defenders were out of the play, which left Dylan all alone when he met the puck perfectly and went in on a breakaway, the Hornets right winger in hot pursuit.

The crowd roared, excited at the suddenness of the play. Dylan faked a backhand, firing a low wrist shot to the stick side. The goalie kicked out his right leg, just managing to get a piece of it. The rebound came straight out. The Hornets winger, so intent on catching Dylan, skated right over the puck, and his clumsy attempt to kick it away sent him tumbling to the ice. After delivering the check that started things off, Matt had followed the play. The puck bounced right to him. He took one step to settle the puck, and then let rip a hard, high shot. The goalie had dropped to his knees, and the puck eluded his outstretched glove hand, tucking under the crossbar for a goal.

Cheers rained down as the Rebels pounded Matt on the helmet. He came over to the bench. "Welcome back to hockey," Charlie said, whacking him on the back.

Zachary came close to scoring on the same shift, taking a neat pass from Matt and firing a slapshot from just inside the top of the right circle. The puck nicked the goalie's shoulder and deflected into the crowd.

"Let's change 'em up," Charlie said.

"Come on, boys," his grandfather said, giving each boy a tap on the helmet as they filed out.

The faceoff was to the goalie's right. The opposing centre was already lined up — well balanced and in good position with his legs wide apart, bent over at the waist. He was small, though; time for Charlie's favourite faceoff play. Charlie tapped his stick twice. Pudge and Jonathon tapped back once. The idea was for Charlie to ignore the puck and tie up his man. Pudge would come off his wing, dig the puck out from Charlie's feet, and shoot. Jonathon's responsibility was to charge the net and screen the goalie.

The referee held the puck over the dot and dropped it. Charlie blocked the centre's stick, then turned into him to shield the puck, pushing him backwards. Pudge gathered the puck as planned and Jonathon drove to the net. Charlie spun inside his man and took a step towards the inside post. Pudge hesitated with the puck, the left defenceman dropping to his knees to block the shot. Instead of shooting, Pudge slid a hard pass to Charlie, who, rather than try to stop it, simply angled his stick for a deflection.

The goalie butterflied in anticipation, but Pudge's pass fooled him. He could only look on helplessly as the puck fluttered end over end into the gaping net. Charlie pumped his fist in the air. Jonathon put his arm around his shoulders.

"Perfect timing, man. That was sweet."

"Way to tie him up in front," he said.

Pudge punched Charlie's glove.

"Great pass."

"Great deflection."

Clang! Clang! Clang!

Danielle stood on her seat, ringing the cowbell, holding a box of popcorn. He wanted to wave to her again, but thought it might look like he was showing off. No need to fire the Hornets up by acting too confident.

The rest of the first and then the second period went equally well. Martin faced a few easy shots. Most of the play was in the Hornets' end. Toward the end of the second, Zachary got behind the defence, taking a perfect pass from Scott. The lanky right winger made no mistake, deking to his backhand, faking to his forehand, then flipping a backhander over the confused goalie's glove.

The buzzer sounded shortly after Zachary's goal. The Rebels crowded around Charlie at their bench.

"Good work, boys," he said. "Let's keep being first to the puck. We have a foot speed advantage. Keep controlling the puck. Love the way we're playing in their end. Forecheck hard. We just need to be careful about getting caught deep in their zone. One quick pass and it's a three-on-two. We're up 3–zip. Play good D and the game's ours."

"Their defence is slow," Scott said. "Forwards, get right on them. They'll turn the puck over. Trust me."

"And make sure we keep the shifts short," Pudge said.

"Don't get tired out there," Nick said. "Up and down and switch it up."

"That's huge for us," Charlie said.

He pulled Pudge aside.

"I'm noticing Matt looks tired. He hasn't played much lately. Maybe we should put you on his line, so you can help with the defence?"

"Makes sense to me," Pudge agreed.

Charlie tapped his shin pads. "Is this not the coolest? Hawks never came close to winning."

"Game's not over," Pudge said quietly.

"We keep bringing it hard, and it will be."

He raced over to the bench to tell Zachary to switch lines.

18

SWING AND A PRAYER

The ref blew his whistle to start the third period. "Rebels, you're looking at a delay-of-game penalty if you don't line up," the referee said. "I'm dropping the puck in five seconds whether you're here or not."

"Coming," Charlie said. "I think it's my line, right Matt?"

Matt was already sitting on the bench. Charlie raced to the circle. Before he could even set up, the ref dropped the puck, and the Hornets centre pulled it back to his defence.

Zachary and Jonathon stayed with their wings, so Charlie went forward to pressure. The defenceman saw that he had to make a quick move, and he made the worse possible decision. Instead of a simple pass across to his defence partner, he tried to thread it past Charlie to his centreman. The puck nicked Charlie's skate and bounced to the side. Charlie reined it in, cutting hard to the net. Neither defenceman was particularly fast. In two strides he had left them behind, and was in alone.

At the hash marks he faked a shot, a move that almost made the goalie drop to his knees. He managed to stay up, but was off balance and now too far out of his net to guard against the deke. Charlie faked a backhand move, then swung to the outside on the forehand, sliding the puck in on the stick side.

He raised his stick high, pumping his arms several times. He rarely celebrated too much after a goal, but at the moment he was too stoked to contain his emotions. The cowbell rang out. Danielle was standing on her seat, going crazy. Hockey was fun again.

"I knew we'd score if we were on the same line," Zachary said, tapping his helmet with his glove.

"Awesome job," Jonathon said. "That should take the fight out of them."

"We can't let up," Charlie said. "One more goal and the game is definitely ours."

The pace of the game began to pick up. Charlie noticed his teammates were changing very quickly, sometimes after twenty seconds. Worse, they were getting very little pressure on the forecheck, which allowed the Hornets to gain the neutral zone at top speed.

About five minutes into the period, after a long shift, Charlie turned to the bench for a change. Matt hopped the boards, just in time to meet a Hornets forward with the puck. Charlie waited for Matt to make a big hit. Instead, he waved at him weakly with his stick. The Hornets forward ended up with a point-blank shot from the top of the circle. Only Martin's quick glove save kept it out.

Matt promptly headed to the bench, his stick across his knees. His face was pale and drawn. He looked as if he was about to faint.

"You all right?" Charlie asked.

Without answering, Matt sat on the bench, and bent deeply gasping for air.

"Matt! What's wrong? You get hurt?"

Matt raised his head, elbows on his knees. "Just winded." He was breathing heavily. "Out of shape. I'll be good. Give me a minute. Take this shift."

Charlie returned to the ice. He could have used a rest.

"Is Matt banged up?" Pudge asked.

He shook his head. "He's cool. Just needs a breather." He didn't have time to say more.

The referee blew his whistle. "Number eight, I'm tired of waiting for your team to line up. Next time you're going to get a penalty."

He hustled over for the draw, but he wasn't focused and lost it cleanly. The Hornets defenceman slapped a low, hard shot on the net. Martin had come out to challenge and handled it easily, kicking his left pad out to deflect the puck to the corner. Scott got to it first. Charlie assumed he would carry the puck behind the net, so he circled deep in the slot to the right to be in position for a breakout pass up the middle. Scott didn't move, however. He blasted the puck off the glass up the left side. The Hornets defenceman tried to block it with his body, but it nicked the boards and ricocheted down the ice.

Charlie stopped at the blue line. He'd let someone else chase it down. His legs were dead, and he wanted a break. Unfortunately, not a single Rebel answered the call. Anticipating an icing, they remained in their own end, most bent over double. Apart from Charlie, they didn't notice that the puck was on net, and the goalie had to play it. He fired the puck back all the way to the Rebels' blue line, where an equally alert winger carried it in.

"Wake up, guys," Charlie yelled.

They had congregated around the net, most resting their sticks across their knees. Charlie was closest, and he raced over to stop the Hornets attacker. He struggled valiantly, but his legs were burning and the player gained the angle. From fifteen feet out, under virtually no pressure, he blasted a rising snap shot over Martin's shoulder and into the net.

Charlie felt like smashing his stick. Had everyone fallen asleep?

"We can't give him that shot. Where's the hustle?" He looked at his teammates' faces. They were exhausted, barely able to stand up straight. They'd played their hearts out — and there was nothing left in the tank. Screaming at them wouldn't help.

"Ref, we'll take a time out," Charlie said.

He skated to the bench, followed by his worn out teammates. When he tried to talk, he found he was breathing too heavily and had to wait a few moments. He was more tired than he thought. The effort on the last play had drained what little energy he had left. What should they do? Maybe they'd gone out too fast, underestimating the Hornets' manpower advantage. The Hornets coach had rolled his lines, gambling that the Rebels, while a more talented group, would eventually tire. That gamble looked good now.

"Our energy level is at zero," he said. "Forget the offence for a while. Get the puck to the red line and fire it in — icing is okay too. We need to kill the clock. One forechecker at the most; everyone else clogs the neutral zone. This is Operation Defend. We can't afford to get caught up-ice. We can hold out if we play carefully in our own end."

"It's gut-check time," Scott said. "Let's eat the pain and win this baby."

"We're still up," Zachary said. "No more easy goals against."

"Matt, take another breather. My line'll start," Charlie said.

As they skated to the faceoff, Charlie told Zachary, "A coach would have helped. We needed to pace ourselves."

Zachary nodded. His face was flushed and his breathing was laboured. Zachary never seemed to get tired. If he was hurting, Charlie had serious doubts about whether they could hold onto the lead.

The rest of the game was a nightmare. The puck rarely left the Rebels' end. Matt tried gamely, but he was finished. Charlie double-shifted for most of the period. Even though they were at even strength, the Rebels played as if they were killing a penalty, icing the puck at every chance and giving little thought to offence. At the seven-minute mark, the Hornets scored to get within two. Two minutes later they counted another off a face-off in the Rebels' zone. Charlie had lost the draw cleanly, and the winger blasted a laser-like slapshot between Martin's pads.

The Hornets kept up the pressure, and came close to tying it up several times. With forty seconds to go, after an icing call against the Rebels, the Hornets pulled their goalie for an extra attacker. The Hornets' supporters clapped and cheered their team on. The Rebels' supporters were quiet, fearing the worst.

The Hornets' centre carried it into the Rebels' zone. Charlie tried to catch him, but he was so tired he could hardly move. The puck slid back to the Hornets right defenceman against the boards. He promptly fired it across the blue line to his defence partner who promptly one-timed it at the net.

Clank.

The puck bounced off the post. Charlie almost felt sorry for the Hornets. That made three goal posts in the third period, and they'd also missed a bunch of easy chances. Christopher flicked the puck up the boards. Zachary was too slow to get there, and the puck dribbled to the point. The defenceman hesitated, and then passed it down low to the left winger. He immediately curled into the slot and whipped a beautiful pass to the right defenceman bearing down on goal.

Martin was screened and out of position. The Hornets player reared back and let it fly. Charlie thought it was a sure goal, when at the last second Robert threw himself in front of the powerful blast. The puck hit him just over the knee and spun back to the blue line. The other defenceman raced over and raised his stick for a slapshot. Charlie summoned every last bit of energy and swung his stick at the puck. The shooter's stick smacked him full on the facemask.

Charlie heard the crowd roar. He turned to look back at his net. Martin was leaning against the crossbar. Robert was still lying on the ice holding his knee. Where was the puck? Charlie was still looking around when Zachary pulled him to his feet.

"What happened?" he asked stupidly.

"Puck's in the net, dude," Zachary said, his lopsided grin firmly in place.

"I can't believe they scored," Charlie said.

"Not your best goal," Jonathon said, "but maybe the sweetest."

He shook his head, unable to follow. "What do you mean, my goal?"

"Take a look, dude," Zachary said, pointing at the Hornets' net.

Charlie's desperate swing had connected, and the puck had miraculously slid the length of the ice and into the net. "Don't tell me we're actually going to win," he said.

"I'm afraid so, bud," Zachary said.

Charlie skated over to Robert. He was gingerly flexing his knee.

"That took reckless to a new level," he said. "Thanks for winning the game for us."

"The team won, not me."

Charlie helped him to his feet. He gave his helmet a tap.

"You're right," he said. "But it takes players like you for a team to win." He put his arm under Robert's elbow. "You need help getting off?"

"I'm good," Robert said.

Charlie admired his courage. No way this tough defenceman was going to let someone carry him off. Charlie would have liked to go off too. Matt had his head down on the bench, so he had to stay on. With a two-goal lead, Charlie was content to let his scowling opponent win the draw. He dropped back to defend against a final charge. The Hornets players stormed down the ice and almost got another goal in the final ten seconds, when the buzzer sounded.

"Woo-hoo!" Scott put his arm across Charlie's back. "The Rebels are undefeated," he crowed.

Charlie laughed. They'd already done something Dunn's team couldn't do — they'd won a game! Granted, it wasn't pretty. They'd have to learn to pace themselves. Conditioning was a huge problem, and they'd have to be better organized. Against the stronger teams in the league they'd have to take their game to another level — and they needed to practise. Still, it was totally awesome to win; and they'd done it all themselves.

Pudge came over and held up his glove. Charlie reached up and gave it a punch. "Relax, Joyce. Lots of time to worry about the next game — for now, just enjoy this win."

He put an arm across Pudge's shoulders.

"I figured out the colour of our sweaters," he said.

"Yeah?" Pudge said.

"It's championship rose."

"You've lost it again, dude."

Charlie gave Pudge's helmet a whack, and Pudge responded with a light punch to his ribs. Together they skated off the ice. Charlie could hear his teammates celebrating on their way to the dressing room. He didn't feel tired at all now. He felt like he could play another game — well, almost.

The Rebels were undefeated. How cool was that?

19

SUDS

The sound of grinding wheels caught his attention, and as he turned towards the sound he saw Zachary flying down the hill on his long board, hands behind his back, holding what looked like a piece of wood.

"Yo, Zachary. Slow down or you'll get a speeding ticket."

He did a big curve to stop. "Got a present for you, dude," Zachary said. He dropped the piece of wood to the pavement and kicked it, and it rolled over to him. "Not the newest model, and it's a bit hacked up. I asked my bro and he said he didn't need it. It's a pretty quick board. The wheels are a bit too hard for my taste — they're like an 85A — gotta be careful on turns big time and slow down cause you can seriously drift. And maybe the wheels are a little small. Good for quick starts though. The bushings are kind of shot, but a little oiling and they'll be cool."

Charlie picked it up and spun the wheels a few times. The wheels were worn and the deck had definitely seen better days. The rails were scratched and big chunks were missing from the nose. He didn't care, though. It was a long board. Now he could race with his friends on The Hill, or keep up when they went for a ride.

"Zachary, thanks. That's totally cool." He hesitated before adding, "Are you sure it's okay? I mean, are you sure your brother doesn't need it . . . ?"

"The dude's got like five boards. He wants you to have it."

Charlie was totally blown away. He held out his fist and Zachary punched it.

"We'd better hustle," Charlie said. "We're late already."

Zachary set off down the hill. Charlie picked up his short board and hopped onto the long board to follow. He couldn't believe the difference in acceleration.

"I see the guys at the gas station," Zachary said over his shoulder.

Charlie merely nodded in reply. He had to concentrate. He wasn't used to this kind of speed. Zachary pulled in first, and Charlie rolled in behind and stopped next to Pudge.

"You've finally decided to join the long board world," Pudge said.

Charlie flashed a grin. "Not the latest model, but Zachary's brother had an extra."

"Cool. I was getting tired of waiting for you all the time."

"Me too," Charlie said, and they both laughed. "Nice of Mr. Stanton to let us use his gas station."

Pudge held his hands out. "Just another satisfied customer at Bruno's Bistro."

Charlie looked up to the sky. "Perfect weather. Who wouldn't want their car washed by the members of the famous Terrence Falls Rebels?"

"We could use the money," Pudge said. "Brent can get us team helmets for around eighty bucks each. That's a serious discount, but once you add the tax, it still comes out to about a thousand dollars. Every bit will help."

"Helmets would be nice," Zachary said. "Right now we look like we're from ten different teams."

Matt, Scott and Nick joined them.

"How much have we raked in so far?" Charlie asked.

"Forty dollars," Pudge said.

"Halfway to a helmet," Zachary said.

Julia and two other girls crossed the street and walked towards them. "Hi guys," Julia said. "What're you up to?"

As soon as they got close, Jonathon sent a short blast of water at them, which garnered screams of protest.

"Thought you were a car," Jonathon said. "Sorry about that."

Julia grabbed a clean towel from a bucket and wiped her face dry. "Very funny. Now, why are you hanging out at Stanton's Gas Station on a Saturday morning?"

"We just love the gas station atmosphere — all that drippy oil," Scott said.

"Looks to me like a fundraiser," Julia said.

"Okay, we're busted," Jonathon said. "Car wash fundraiser it is."

"How's it going?" she said.

"We were just discussing finances. We've amassed forty dollars to date," Jonathon answered.

She whistled. "In how long?"

"Two days," Scott said.

The girls laughed.

"I'm being rude," Julia said. "I think some of you may know Rebecca from school. And this is Alexandra. She's new in Terrence Falls."

They all said hi. Charlie had seen Rebecca before. She'd played on the Terrence Falls hockey team with Julia. Alexandra was an attractive girl, quite tall, but maybe not as pretty as Julia. As usual, Charlie was tongue-tied around the girls, but Jonathon and Scott had no such problem and kept the girls laughing with a steady stream of jokes. Two more cars came, and Charlie busied himself with washing and drying. When no one was looking, Julia hooked up a spare hose and took revenge by dousing Jonathon. Charlie laughed and turned to wave to a departing customer. That's when a blast of cold water hit his back.

He spun around. Julia and her friends were doubled over.

"Why me? I'm innocent!" he said.

"You're all guilty," Julia said, and she promptly sprayed him again. Everyone was laughing now.

"We should get going. Have fun, boys," Julia said.

Charlie went to dry himself off. Julia came over. "What time do you play tonight?" she asked as Charlie was folding some towels.

"Game's at 7:30."

"I play at 6:00. I'll stick around and watch."

"Great. It should be a real test — the Snow Birds."

"Good luck."

He waved to her as she left, and then braced himself for some ribbing as Scott came over.

"You ever seen Alexandra before?" he asked.

Charlie shook his head. "Why?"

"No reason. I thought she looked familiar."

"Did she look like a girlfriend?"

Scott gave Charlie a good-natured shove. "Maybe," he said. "Maybe."

Scott tossed a soapy sponge at Nick, who picked up a dirty bucket of water. He was about to toss it when Charlie intervened.

Business began to pick up and they washed a bunch of cars. Then a large, black truck sped over the curb, bouncing slightly, and skidded to a halt.

The screeching tires startled Charlie, and tinted windows made it impossible to see inside. Charlie's heart sank when Jake, Thomas, Liam and Roscoe spilled out.

Through the driver's side window a deep voice instructed them to "Make it shine, boys." The window closed and the door opened.

Charlie guessed he was Jake's father. He had his son's jet-black hair and broad shoulders. He wore sunglasses, which he lifted to his forehead. A cigar burned between his thick fingers. As he closed the door a beer can tumbled to the pavement. He picked it up and tossed it back in the car.

"That was weird," he whispered to Pudge.

"I hear he drinks a bit too much," Pudge whispered back. "My dad . . . I heard him talking to my mom . . ."

Jake's father spotted Pudge. He came over and shook his hand. "Nice to see you again, son. You haven't been around much lately since you aren't playing for the Wildcats. Is your dad well?"

"He's doing good," Pudge replied.

Charlie could smell the beer on his breath. For the first time he actually felt sorry for Jake. Must be tough to have a father who drinks.

"Glad to hear it. Got to get to his restaurant again one of these days. Great guy — the best. Send him my regards." He looked to his left. "Is that Mr. Danko?" He took a deep puff on his cigar. "Where've you been hiding?"

Matt shuffled his feet, clearing his throat a few times. "I've been real busy lately."

"Well, don't be a stranger. I remember when you used to practically live at our house. Speaking of which, your old man was helping me out not too long ago. I have some more work for him. My basement is a total mess. I need it cleaned out. Tell him I'll call. I've been out of town on business, but I'll make some time. Tell him, okay?"

Matt's face was beet red. "Okay," he said.

Jake's dad blew a smoke ring. "So who're you playing hockey for this year?"

"Playing with these guys — the Rebels. This is a team fundraiser."

"That's cool. I'm glad I stopped. Glad to help out. Jake was filling me in. You're like an expansion team. Might not win too many games this year. But hey, hockey's supposed to be for fun, right?" He laughed deeply and winked.

Charlie had mixed feelings. Jake's dad didn't seem like such a bad guy. But then why embarrass Matt like that in front of all the guys?

"I'm just gonna get some mints inside," Jake's dad

said. "Jakey, why don't you catch up with your buds?" He walked inside the garage.

The two groups faced each other. Charlie worried about a brawl. Mr. Stanton would be furious.

"This whole feud thing is getting stale," he said, hoping to defuse the tension. "We'll just wash this car, and you can go on your way. Save your trash talk for another day."

"Joyce, you always underestimate me," Jake said. "I wanted to say how much I admire your courage . . . yes, that's the word . . . your courage . . . for starting up the Rebels. I was saying that to Liam not five minutes ago, wasn't I, Liam?"

"Absolutely. It might even have been three minutes," Liam said.

Charlie didn't respond. If he reacted, his friends would do the same, and a fight would be inevitable.

"I hear your sweaters have a unique design — and what colour would you say they are?" Jake asked.

"A brilliant pink, I believe," Liam said.

"Technically, I think it's ballet pink," Jake said.

"Whatever colour, it makes you sick to look at them," Thomas said.

"Not as sick as watching them play," Roscoe said.

That broke them up.

"Jake, you're a broken record," Charlie said.

"And you'll have a broken neck after our game on Sunday," Jake said.

"Why don't we settle it now?" Scott said.

"Forget him," Charlie said. "He's not worth the effort."

"I'd like to oblige you, dude, but not with Dad

around," Jake said. "But I'll be sure to run your head through the boards, just for old times' sake."

Charlie, Dylan and Zachary finished washing the truck.

Scott snorted in disgust and walked away, wringing out a wet towel. Charlie knew what Scott really wanted to wring out!

Jake's father returned.

"Matt and Pudge, really nice to see you again. Hope you can come by the house," he said. The two boys nodded.

"Here's ten bucks for the wash. Looks like you did a bang-up job. Thanks."

They watched in silence as the truck pulled away.

"I say rip that money up. It might have touched Jake," Scott said.

"Second that," Matt said.

Charlie ignored their suggestion. It would be pointless.

"Car," Pudge shouted.

Charlie wandered over with the towels. His English teacher and former hockey coach stepped out.

"This must be my lucky day," Hilton said. "I was just thinking about how I'd find the time to clean this filthy vehicle, and I come across a fine crop of hockey players providing that very service."

"Step aside, Mr. Hilton," Charlie said. "We'll get this done in no time."

The arrival of his former coach made him forget about what had just happened. Everyone seemed in good spirits as they washed the car. The twins sprayed the outside. Next, Scott, Nick and Matt attacked it with large foamy sponges. The twins gave it another soaking, and Charlie, Pudge, Zachary and Dylan dried it off.

Hilton caught Charlie's eye.

"How's the team doing?" he asked.

He stopped drying and stood up.

"We won our first game against the Hornets — barely, but we won. We also beat the Tornadoes 3–0. We lost to the Tigers 5–3, but it was close. The next two games will be the real test. Tonight we play the Snow Birds, and then the Wildcats on Sunday."

"Sounds as if you're off to a solid start."

"We could use a few more guys. We tend to run out of steam by the third period, what with only two forward lines. The Snow Birds will kill us if we slow down. I think we need to play defensive, conserve our energy until later in the game. Otherwise, we could be in trouble."

"Can I make a suggestion?"

"Of course."

By this time the others had formed a semi-circle around Hilton.

"Send the puck in deep as often as you can, and only one forechecker. The other two forwards line up across the blue line, the defence a bit back. I've seen them play. Their defencemen love to rush. Stop them before they get going and force some passes. Clog the middle and make them go outside. You should get some good chances off turnovers."

"I think we're finished your car," Pudge said.

Hilton examined it. "Looks great. So what's the cost for this service?"

"We accept any size donation," Scott said, "and

have I ever mentioned what an amazing privilege it was to have such a superb tactician behind the bench for the high school hockey tournament?"

"Easy does it, Scott," Hilton said, laughing.

"It's ten dollars," Charlie said, giving Scott a dirty look.

Hilton pulled out his wallet and handed Charlie a twenty-dollar bill.

"I'll get you the change."

"That's okay. Good luck in your game tonight," he said, getting in his car and driving off.

Elated by his teacher's generosity, Charlie counted the money they'd made so far — $285. At this rate, by the end of the day, they'd easily be more than halfway to paying off the helmets. Another car pulled in. Things were definitely beginning to look up.

20

HIT THE WALL

Charlie watched the Snow Birds as he rounded centre. They were intimidating. J.C. Savard was firing shots at the backup goalie. The Rebels would have to shut him down or there'd be little chance of winning. Only five games into the regular season and he already had a big lead in the scoring race. Burnett was stretching by his bench. The big, rangy defender was a deadly scorer in his own right. And if that weren't enough, their acrobatic goalie, Alexi Tolstoy, busy scraping his goal crease, had let in only one goal this season.

As he circled behind the goal he spotted Julia with Alexandra and Rebecca. Julia waved, and he waved back. He noticed some kids from school in the crowd. Nice of them to support the team, he thought. He picked up some speed, found a puck, and flicked it in the air, bouncing it off the blade a few times. He felt silly showing off, but why not? The nerves were kicking in and it took his mind off the game.

Bhrrr!

They all took a few final laps after the buzzer and then crowded around Martin.

"This is it," Charlie said. "We've worked hard to get

here. Got some wins, but they mean nothing if we can't bring it tonight. The Snow Birds were last year's champions. Let's show them who's going to win it this year. Gloves in the middle, boys."

Their gloves piled on top of Charlie's.

"Go, Rebels, go!" they chanted, tossing their gloves in the air.

The crowd was getting excited, clapping and cheering for both teams.

"Go for it, Charlie!"

That sounded like Julia. He forced himself to focus. His line was starting. J.C. Savard was waiting at centre.

"Have a good one," Savard said, tapping Charlie on the shin pads with his stick.

"You too," he said, bending down for the draw.

He wanted to establish himself physically right off the bat. When the puck dropped he tied Savard's stick up and pushed hard into him. Savard was caught off guard. He fell back, which allowed Charlie to kick the puck to Scott.

Good start, he thought, spinning to his right, looking for a pass. Instead, Scott feinted his way and fired it across the blue line to Nick. Charlie quickly changed directions, and Nick slipped a pass to him just over the red line. He cut sharply on his right skate and headed up ice. For a moment he was tempted to try to split the defence. Hilton had warned them about getting caught. Rather than risk turning the puck over in the neutral zone, he fired it into the right corner and continued in on the forecheck.

He glanced back with satisfaction. Zachary and Jonathon were also following Hilton's advice — standing at the blue line with Scott and Nick plugging the middle. Burnett had retrieved the puck. Charlie closed in, determined to make him pass. Burnett retreated behind his net, standing tall to survey the scene. Without warning, he took off to his right. Charlie wasn't fooled. He shifted across, laying his stick along the ice to cut off the passing lane. Burnett dumped it off to his right winger. Charlie merely continued that way and lowered his shoulder, crushing the puck carrier into the boards. Burnett snuck in and retrieved the puck, with Charlie close behind. Burnett decided to set up again and went back behind his net.

Charlie settled in the slot and waited. This time Savard circled behind the net and took the puck. Charlie skated over, forcing Savard to drop it to the trailing Burnett. Then, to the delight of the Rebels supporters, Charlie poke-checked Burnett before he could take two steps. The speedy defenceman recovered quickly and retreated to the safety of his net.

Charlie guessed Burnett would try to leg it out himself. He passed to his defence partner in the left corner. Charlie pretended to follow, never taking his eye off Burnett. Sure enough, the puck came back, and Burnett promptly skated up the right side.

Charlie met him at the top of the circle. Zachary stepped up also. Cornered, and with nowhere to go, Burnett tried a wild pass to Savard up the middle. Nick was right on him, and the puck jumped over Savard's stick and down the ice.

The Rebels supporters roared their approval, clapping and chanting, "Re-bels! Re-bels! Re-bels!"

Tweet.

The ref's whistle signaled icing. Charlie headed to the bench.

"Keep up the pressure," he said, as Matt jumped over the boards to take his place.

"Awesome shift, boys," he said on the bench. "We play a disciplined game and we'll be in this. The turnovers will come. Get the first goal, and this game's ours."

Charlie was excited to see the old Matt back — aggressive on the puck, strong at both ends, lightning fast, and ready to play the body. After a dump-in by Dylan, he delivered a massive hit. The defenceman crumpled to the ice, holding his ribs. The whistle stopped play. The Rebels players drifted to the bench to wait for him to recover.

"Way to get in there, Matt," Charlie said. "I'm lovin' this defensive coverage. We're playing smart hockey. They're totally confused."

"One shift at a time," Matt said, slightly winded from the hit also. "No letting up — not one second. These guys are no big deal."

"Let's keep the energy level high for the first half of this period, and then settle back," Charlie said.

"We can play these guys," Matt said. "Don't be intimidated. You hit them — they fall. It's simple."

"Forwards are playing awesome," Scott said, slapping Matt's shin pads. "They can't make a move. I haven't had to do anything yet — and I'm liking that big time."

The Snow Birds player got up slowly and, with the help of two teammates, skated to his bench. Players from both teams banged their sticks on the ice. The crowd clapped politely.

Matt's line stayed on for the faceoff. He won the draw back to Scott, whose one-timer nearly beat Alexi. The Snow Birds showed how good a team they were, however. The centre didn't let Matt get to the net, and the right defenceman in front tied up Pudge so he couldn't get the rebound. The other defender slapped the puck out of harm's way. The left winger carried it up to the hash marks and then chipped it off the wall and out of the zone, relieving the pressure.

The rest of the period went according to plan. The Rebels didn't score, although they had some chances, and the Snow Birds didn't score either. Charlie couldn't have been happier. They were in the game; and better yet, the Snow Birds couldn't crack their defensive scheme. Martin barely worked up a sweat. Time and again the Snow Birds turned the puck over in the neutral zone, or they iced the puck after forcing a pass.

"I'm feeling it, boys," Scott said, as they changed ends for the second period. "They're freaked. I'm telling you. They don't have a clue. Just keep dumping it in and forechecking like mad."

"No penalties is huge," Pudge said. "We can't give them a power play."

"Pudge is right," Charlie said. "We didn't have a penalty that period. Even strength we can play with them — no problem."

His line was up. Charlie had to wait at centre because the Snow Birds were still huddled around their coach. He was drawing a play on a clipboard, poking his black marker forcefully several times. The referee's whistle interrupted, and they filed onto the bench, with Savard coming out for the faceoff. The ref dropped the puck too hard, and it bounced higher than usual. Both players missed it, their sticks striking each other instead. It bounced to Charlie's left and he was able to whack it between the Snow Birds defencemen and down the ice. The Rebels fans went crazy. They loved seeing Charlie beat the great J.C. Savard on a faceoff.

"Sharpen your skates, Savard. You're looking clumsy out there."

"It's only gonna get worse, Snow Birds."

Alexi stopped the puck behind his net, leaving it for Burnett. Charlie set up for the forecheck. What happened next took him, and his linemates, completely by surprise.

Savard swung behind the net and carried the puck up the right side. Charlie shifted across to cut him off. Unlike during the first period, Savard skated as hard as he could and made no attempt to pass to the right winger. Instead, once Charlie had committed, he dropped it back to Burnett. Charlie peeled over, but before he could get close, Burnett slid a pass to his left winger cutting in from the boards, who in turn hit Savard breaking out up the middle. The Snow Birds fans started to make some noise — finally their team had broken through the Rebels defence unhindered. Savard darted to his left to keep away from Christopher, who had pressed forward. Robert had stayed back, however. That left a seam between them. Savard cut back to the right, shrugging off Christopher's stick check. From there it was a footrace. Robert tried valiantly, but Savard was too fast and by the blue line he was in alone.

Ten feet from the net Savard cut right, the puck on his forehand. Savard then swept his stick across the crease — except the puck wasn't on his stick. Martin fell for the fake, dropping to his knees to cover the right side. Savard even pretended to take a backhand. The puck slid, untouched, inside the left post.

Charlie slapped the boards with his stick. That forecheck had been totally lame. He'd allowed them to get the puck out of their zone at top speed, something that hadn't happened once the entire first period.

The Rebels quickly learned that the first period strategy was no longer working. The Snow Birds used quick passes to get past the first forechecker, and then hit the man cutting up the middle. At the eight-minute mark of the second period, Savard set up another goal, breaking across the line and finding Burnett with a perfect pass at the top of the right circle. He buried a blast low to the stick side to make it 2–0.

Charlie was on the bench at the time.

"Zachary, Jonathon, we need to change things up. They're killing us with the centre circling the net and dropping it to the defenceman. One forechecker can't cover both players. Let's go with two forecheckers in deep and stop the play before it develops. We need to stop the breakout pass up the middle."

"But if we miss, don't we risk an odd-man rush?" Jonathon said.

He was right — but what else could they do? Charlie had no time to consider. He needed to tell the defence what they were doing, and someone had to tell the other forward line.

"We'll just try it," he said. "I think it'll work."

He shifted down the bench to tell Scott and Nick. Christopher dumped the puck in deep, and the twins, tired after a long shift, came over for a change. Scott and Nick went out before he had a chance to talk to them. On his way back, Zachary and Jonathon changed for Dylan and Pudge. "Just great," he said to himself. Scott and Nick had no idea what Zachary and Jonathon were going to do. But at least he could tell the rest of his teammates.

"Listen up," he said to the players on the bench.

"Centre! Centre!" Matt yelled. He was coming off for a change.

Charlie had to go on. As planned, Zachary and Jonathon pressured the Snow Birds defence. Charlie stayed back and picked up a check. Good thing too, because the defenceman with the puck saw the two wingers coming. He shouted to the centre, who, instead of circling the net, cut up the middle. A quick pass and he was storming towards the Rebels' end.

To make matters worse, Scott and Nick were in the middle of the neutral zone, as they had been all game. Charlie tried to cut him off but the centre was too quick, and he sent a crisp pass to the left winger streaking down the boards. Nick was caught flatfooted, and the forward had a clear cut breakaway almost from centre. At the hash marks, he froze Martin with a quick feint and then snapped a hard wrist shot to the stick side, just over the blocker. Martin barely moved. The puck sneaked under the crossbar, ricocheting off the inside support bar, knocking Martin's water bottle to the ice before bouncing straight out. At first Charlie thought it had hit the crossbar. The ref was right there, however. He blew his whistle and pointed at the net. As he circled around, Charlie smashed his stick on the post.

The shaft snapped in two. He threw it in disgust against the boards.

"Awesome shot, man," he heard the Snow Birds centre say.

"The dude didn't even move," said another player.

"He didn't even see it," the goal scorer boasted.

They all laughed, slapping gloves.

Charlie felt like smashing the goal scorer to the ice. The guy was so full of himself. He picked up his broken stick.

Zachary had skated over to him. "Hey, dude, you need to keep cool. We're still in the game."

He suddenly felt ridiculous. He'd just broken a three hundred-dollar stick!

"Sorry, Zachary. I just lost it. I'm good. But how messed was that?"

"I thought you told the defence what we were doing."

"I tried but they went out before . . ." He stopped. "Ref, can we get a time out?"

The referee blew his whistle. "Time out . . . Red . . . ?" He looked at Charlie. "Your sweater is red, right?"

He was in no mood for jokes about the colour of his sweater. He nodded and went to the bench. Then he explained the new forechecking strategy.

"Let's try to slow them down," Pudge said quietly.

"We're letting them take it to us," Scott said. "We gotta be more aggressive."

"Crank up the heat again," Matt said. "First to the puck every time."

A few more clichés were offered, but Charlie could see that no one really believed they could win — and neither did he. The team's confidence was shattered, and the game became a laugher for the Snow Birds. The puck barely left the Rebels' zone, as if the Snow Birds were on a perpetual power play. Charlie was relieved when the buzzer finally sounded to put an end to his misery. The final score was 7–0 — a massacre.

Charlie was so embarrassed he couldn't look the Snow Birds players in the eye when shaking hands. He skated to the bench to help carry the extra sticks.

"Can you think of something good to say after that?" Pudge asked. He reached for an empty water bottle.

"How about we were lucky to lose by seven."

"Not very inspirational."

"I don't feel inspired."

Pudge punched him lightly on the shoulder pads. "It's not your fault, Charlie."

"I couldn't think of any adjustments. Hilton's strategy worked perfectly in the first period. When they changed their breakout, I couldn't get the guys organized. I ended up making things worse, confusing everyone. I still don't know what we should have done — how inspiring is that? What about the next time we play them? The score'll be 20–0."

"We could've used a coach, for sure," Pudge said. "It's tough to play and coach at the same time."

"What am I supposed to do?"

"I'm not saying you have to do anything. We were all supposed to do the coaching, not just you. It's just . . . maybe we have to divide jobs up, and be more organized at the beginning of the game."

"How were we not organized?"

"I don't know. Like maybe we need a better system for changing strategies. We could huddle up at the end of each period. That would give everyone a chance to decide on things."

Charlie had to admit that Pudge was right. "Good idea. Maybe every game we have a defenceman and a forward in charge of our forechecking strategy, or something like that. We can work it out later."

The room was dead quiet when they walked in. No one had even started to undress.

Charlie didn't know what to say — and he didn't have the energy to try. This clearly wasn't the time to talk about coaching. He collapsed onto the bench, tossing his helmet roughly into his bag.

Just then, the door swung open. Bob Dale, the Snow Birds' coach, entered, holding some sticks taped together and a cardboard box that he dropped to the floor.

"Probably not the result you were looking for," he said in a gravelly baritone voice.

Charlie had heard all about this legendary coach. Before coaching the Snow Birds, he'd taken another team from atom all the way to midget, and they'd won the championship practically every year. Two players from that team played in the NHL, and several more played professionally in lower leagues or overseas, or got university scholarships.

"I wanted to applaud your effort," he continued. "You never quit, and I'm telling you, if you'd scored first it might have been a different game. Anyway, all the other teams in the league appreciate what you've done, how much work it must have been, and still is, and we all want to encourage you to keep going. I know a game like this is hard to swallow. But it's only one game. Learn from it, and come out stronger next time."

"Thanks, Mr. Dale," Charlie said. "You've got a great team over there."

"I can tell you that every kid on my team has a tremendous amount of respect for each one of you," he said. "In my books, you're real hockey players, and that's about the highest compliment I can pay." He leaned the sticks against the wall. "Here's a few extra sticks I thought you could use, and a box of tape — on me. Good luck."

"Thanks," Charlie said.

Dale shook Charlie's hand warmly.

"Take care, guys," he said waving as he left, "and keep plugging away."

When the door closed, Scott said, "He's totally scared of us."

Nick snorted. "He's afraid his players will wear themselves out scoring so many goals."

"Come on. He's trying to bribe us with sticks and tape. It's sad."

"Sad was when Savard slipped the puck between your skates and scored on the breakaway," Nick said.

"So where was my defence partner?"

"Totally out of position."

They both laughed.

Everyone's spirits lifted. The normal banter started up again as they got dressed. Charlie kept quiet. He'd seen a real coach in action — his change in strategy after the first period, his kind words and generosity. Who wouldn't love to play for a guy like that? He noticed

Zachary was keeping quiet too. No surprise there. Zachary must be kicking himself. He could have been a part of that amazing team.

A volleyball game with a roll of tape broke out. The tape came to Charlie, and he slapped it across the room. His heart wasn't in it, though. The loss was painful — to be destroyed like that — with all those kids from school watching, including Julia. Just pathetic!

INSPIRATION

Charlie adjusted his scarf to protect his face against the frigid wind. Snowflakes began to fall, adding to his misery. He lowered his head and trudged on towards the rink. He was tired — the early practices were wearing him down. The weather wasn't helping either — not even Christmas yet and it was snowing like crazy. Normally, he walked with Dylan, but he had a special band practice and begged off. Christopher and Zachary had called to say they weren't coming because of schoolwork. He wondered who would be there.

He picked up the pace in a mostly futile effort to stay warm. To his dismay, the arena wasn't much warmer. He blew on his hands as he headed to the dressing room, and pushed the door open.

Pudge was sitting by himself at the far end. A scarf covered his face, and with his bulky hood pulled up all Charlie could see were his eyes peering out.

"You might want to change in the next room," Pudge said. "Not much space in here."

"I'll just squeeze into the other corner." He leaned against the wall and slumped down. He dreaded the feel of the ice-cold equipment on his body. "Is Gus trying to save money on heating?"

"I guess it's so cold outside no amount of heat would make a difference."

"So what's the deal? Anyone e-mail about not coming?"

"Matt said he had homework. Doubt he'll be here. That's it."

Charlie shook his head in disgust. Things had come off the rails since the Snow Birds game. They'd lost their next two, against the Wildcats and the Hornets, and tied the Tigers. Their lone win came against the lowly Tornadoes. Charlie had scored in every game, but everyone else was mired in a slump. Even the reliable Zachary had missed a breakaway against the Hornets, and they ended up losing 4–3 on a heartbreaking goal in the final minute. The loss had been particularly painful because Mike had joined that team. Apparently, his dad had offered the Hornets new equipment and sticks, in order to land his son a spot. As usual, Mike acted like he was a superstar, and taunted the Rebels when the game ended.

"This is pointless," Charlie said.

"How about a rousing game of one-on-one?" Pudge asked.

"We might get slightly bored after an hour."

Pudge stuffed his hands into his pockets. "The practice time is brutal. We could scale it back."

"We only practise once or twice a week as it is!" Charlie thundered. "We all agreed to practise — we made a commitment. It's easy to make excuses. Where is everyone? Why am I hauling my butt out of bed at five in the morning for this?"

"I don't know, Charlie," Pudge said.

"Maybe this was all a dumb idea. It's typical. At first we were all stoked. Now that's over, and no one feels like coming to the rink on a freezing cold day. The Rebels! We should change our name to the Losers."

Pudge cleared his throat and wrapped his arms across his chest. "I don't think this was a dumb idea. You're right about guys slacking off. But the real problem could be playing without a coach. We knew that would be tough. We're all friends. Are we going to bench the guys that missed this practice or make them skate extra laps?"

"So now it's my fault. Why can't those guys be serious once in a while? They're always joking around. Sometimes you've gotta get focused, especially before a game. And we have to practise or we'll never beat anyone."

"I didn't say it was your fault. You've done more for this team than anyone. But maybe we underestimated the coach factor."

Charlie could see from the expression on Pudge's face that he wasn't dissing him. He was just telling the truth. And Pudge was the last guy he should be yelling at. He slumped even lower against the wall.

"Can't say I blame them much. How fun is it to practise at six in the morning in the winter? But we need some discipline, especially on the ice. Guys are hogging the puck, staying out too long, taking bad penalties. I feel like a jerk if I say anything. It's not like I'm perfect."

"We're not even halfway through the season," Pudge added. "It's only going to get worse."

They sat in silence for a minute.

"Think of anything yet?" Charlie said.

"Only that I'd kill to be back in bed. What about you?"

"I have an idea. It's a bit out there — and I don't know if it has any chance of working . . ."

"I already like it — better than freezing to death in this dressing room."

"Hilton!"

Pudge rolled his eyes. "He never coaches minor hockey — only school teams. Don't you think he gets asked every year? He and Dale are the best coaches around. But he's too busy — and I think he and his wife just had a kid. No chance, my friend."

"I know, but we're desperate. What if he did it part time — came to just some games and practices? Anything would be better than this. You got a better idea, cool. If not, then what's the harm in asking?"

"Joyce, I'll say this. You think big."

"No guts, no glory."

"Let's do it."

Charlie slapped his hockey bag. "The way I see it, we have two choices. First, slowly freeze to death in this dressing room, or go back to my place, slam home some bacon, eggs and homefries, and then confront Mr. William Hilton when he foolishly steps out of his car in the school parking lot."

"You're making more sense to me every second."

The cold and the early hour no longer on his mind, Charlie slung his equipment over his shoulder. He forced himself not to get his hopes up. It was a total long shot at best. But what if Hilton said yes?

* * *

They ran over to Hilton's car. It was empty.

"We're such idiots," Charlie said. "Too busy stuffing our faces, and now he's already inside."

"No big deal," Pudge said. "So we go talk to him."

Charlie held up a hand for a high-five. "That's crazy enough to work."

They jogged to the front door and went in. The school was deserted and completely quiet, so much so that it felt as if they were breaking in.

"It's like we're ninja warriors on a mission," Pudge said.

Charlie burst out laughing. "I'm trying to imagine you in a skin-tight black leotard," he said, "and trust me, it wasn't pretty."

"I'd kill you with a death blow, but I don't want to jeopardize the mission."

"Follow me," Charlie said.

They pretended to scale the stairs like ninjas, hopping over the railings and hiding behind doors. Charlie peered into the hallway. "The coast is clear. Target is approximately seven point two five metres away."

He slammed the door open and they both jumped into the hallway — and almost ran into Principal Holmes.

"My goodness, boys. Please be gentle with the doors. They don't grow on trees, you know."

"Sorry, Principal Holmes," Charlie said.

"And please, no running in the hall."

"Okay, Principal Holmes," Pudge said.

"Now, where were you going in such a hurry?"

"We have to speak to Mr. Hilton. We're in his homeroom . . . it's about an English assignment."

Principal Holmes nodded vigorously. "I like your discipline. Well done, boys. I imagine I'll see you in the library shortly."

He nodded a few more times and walked away.

Pudge rolled his eyes, and Charlie had to bite his lip to keep from laughing. Pudge pointed at the door to Hilton's classroom, and suddenly Charlie lost the urge to laugh.

He looked through the classroom window. Hilton was writing on the blackboard. When Charlie knocked, Hilton looked up in surprise, and waved them in.

"Did we arrange to meet this morning?"

"No, Mr. Hilton," Charlie said. "We wanted to talk to you about something. Is this a bad time?"

"Not at all," he said. "Why don't you take a seat?" Charlie and Pudge sat in the front row. Hilton leaned against the desk. "What can I do for you?"

"We . . . well, I . . . or I guess I should say Pudge and I, since Pudge is here . . ."

Get on with it, he told himself. Why was he so nervous?

"Anyway, we wanted to ask your advice about something . . . and maybe ask a favour."

A smile flickered across Hilton's face. "You've got my attention. What's up?"

"It's about the Rebels," he said. "Things were going great — at first, that is. All the guys were totally psyched. We even won a few games. The practices were good too. Then we played the Snow Birds."

"I remember," he said. "You told me at the car wash."

"That's right," he said. "We took your advice, sent

in one forechecker and held everyone else back in the neutral zone. It worked perfectly for the first period, which ended 0–0. Then they started to swing their centre behind the net, supported by both defencemen and the offside winger cutting inside. We couldn't get any pressure. We completely fell apart — lost 7–zip. It was totally ugly."

"It's tough to play that way the whole game," Hilton said. "I would have either sent guys in really deep to disrupt the defence early, or backed off completely."

"That's what we wanted to talk to you about," Charlie said. "We did neither. We sort of did something in between."

"Never a good idea," Hilton said.

"That's for sure," Pudge said. "We barely touched the puck the rest of the game."

"And that's when we realized that playing without a coach was impossible," Charlie said. "You can't play and try to run a team at the same time. I tried to do both — maybe I did a bad job — we all got confused, and ended up doing nothing. Guys lost respect."

"They still respect you," Pudge said.

"Not as a coach," Charlie said, "which I'm not. We need someone on the bench during the games, at the very least. My grandfather's helping out, but he doesn't know hockey. We're desperate."

Hilton folded his arms across his chest. "Have you got any candidates in mind?"

Charlie smiled awkwardly. "I guess I should come to the point. We were wondering — Pudge and I — if you had a little free time, and maybe could help us out, even a little, like during the games, or even home games, or the occasional practice, anything at all . . ." his voice trailed off.

"Where do you play your home games?"

"The Ice Palace," they both said.

"When do you practise?"

"Same place — at six in the morning," Charlie said.

Hilton winced. "That's an ungodly time for practice, isn't it?"

"Yes, sir," Charlie said, "but we don't have a sponsor. Well, we have one, but only for sweaters — The Hockey Shop."

"A great place," Hilton said. "I used to buy my stuff there when I was a kid. The son runs it now. What's his name . . . ?"

"Brent Sanderson."

He nodded. "So he came up with the uniforms."

"That's all he could afford. The rink manager offered us free practice time."

Hilton nodded. "So you've been practising at six o'clock in the morning."

"We started out twice a week." Charlie sighed. "But attendance has been kind of lame lately."

Hilton didn't respond. Finally, he unfolded his arms, and rubbed his palms together. "Guys, I'd really like to help. I would. I think you've taken on quite a responsibility, and have done a fine job. Most kids would have quit long ago, and you should be proud of yourselves regardless of how the season turns out. But I have a baby at home, and my schedule's rather full. I can't tell you how many times I've been approached to coach. I promised my wife that I wouldn't spend my life at the rink."

Charlie cast his eyes to the floor. He felt bad about putting him on the spot. It wasn't fair. He had gotten carried away — a bit selfish.

"No worries," he said, trying to sound cheerful. "We knew you probably couldn't. We just thought if you could help once in a while that would be great. No big deal. Sorry for bothering you. I know you have some work to do. We'll leave you alone. See you in a few minutes when class starts."

He and Pudge got up to leave.

"Did you practise this morning?" Hilton asked quietly.

"We did," Charlie said, "but not a lot of guys were able to make it."

"How many did?"

Charlie's shoulders sagged. "Two."

"Am I looking at them?"

"You are," he admitted.

Hilton ran a hand slowly across his forehead. He leaned back, staring up at the ceiling.

"How many guys can you get out to a practice tomorrow?"

"Tough to say," Charlie said. "Everyone always has an excuse . . ."

"You give me a full team, on the ice at six sharp, and I'll coach."

Charlie and Pudge stared at their teacher.

"Can you do that?" Hilton said. "If guys won't commit, it's no deal."

Charlie wasn't sure exactly what he meant. "How often can you help out?" he asked.

"You either coach or you don't. I'll see you at the

rink. Tell your teammates we practise twice a week —
unless I think we need more — which, from the sounds
of it, we do."

Charlie felt like jumping to his feet and letting out a
scream.

"That's awesome, Mr. Hilton," Charlie said. "I
don't know what to say. The guys are gonna freak."

"Six o'clock sharp — I mean it."

"No problem," Charlie said. "And thanks."

He could hardly believe what was happening.

"One more thing," Hilton said.

"You name it," they said together.

"All the players need to keep up with their school
work — and perhaps even improve. School comes
before hockey."

He knew that was intended for him. His marks had
been suffering lately. He'd done badly on a few assign-
ments. He vowed to cut down on the television and get
his work done.

"You can count on us," he said.

"I know I can," he replied. Hilton picked up a piece
of chalk.

Charlie barely remembered walking back outside.
Zachary was there doing tricks on his board. "Zachary!"
he yelled between cupped hands.

Zachary waved, and with a deft push on the heel of
the board, cut sharply and headed towards them. "Sorry
about practice," he said. "I was up until midnight finishing my science project. Ask me something about
gravity."

"Okay. Who's going to land on you like a ton of
bricks if you don't show up to practice tomorrow?"

"Come on, Charlie. Don't tell me you called another practice. I gotta get some sleep."

"Hey, boys," Scott said, joining them. "Sorry about practice. I slept in. Pathetic excuse, I know. I was trying to come up with a better one. I'd thought of going with the old classic — kidnapped by aliens — but then decided to tell the truth. Forgive me."

"You're forgiven," Charlie said impatiently. "Forget today. We need you both at practice tomorrow."

"There's a practice tomorrow?" Nick said.

"Do you guys pop up out of the ground?" Pudge asked.

"Now, about the practice—" Charlie said.

"What about it?" Matt said. "Sorry about this morning, guys. How'd it go?"

"Can't tell you," Scott said. "Top secret."

"Everyone just shut up for a second — and listen," Charlie said. "Tomorrow we have a practice." They all groaned. "But I didn't call it." He looked around. "Does anyone want to know who did?"

Scott put up his hand. Charlie ignored him. He knew a set up when he saw one.

"Pick me," Scott said. "I know the answer."

Charlie gave in. "Get it over with."

"Aliens have taken over the planet and our new coach, Mr. Zergoth, wants us to work on our defensive zone coverage."

"Not quite," he said. "You're right about one thing, though. Our coach called the practice." That got their attention, with Pudge grinning from ear to ear.

"I'll take this one, boys," Zachary said. "Who's the coach?"

Charlie let his smile do the talking.

Zachary remained unconvinced. "I can't believe it. He doesn't coach minor hockey."

"He does now, dude."

Scott let out a war cry and began dancing around them, arms flailing, bouncing up and down. "Practice, practice, I love practice," he chanted.

They all joined in, Charlie included, dancing, high-fiving, and shouting at the top of their lungs. Passers-by gave them a wide berth. Six guys jumping around like maniacs would scare most people. Charlie couldn't have cared less. The season, so bleak only three hours earlier in that dressing room, was suddenly full of promise. As far as he was concerned a new season had just begun — a second chance.

"Bring on the Snow Birds!" Charlie said. "Bring them all on!"

22

HEADS UP

Charlie slurped deeply from the water bottle and spit some out on the ice. The ice cold water refreshed his entire body. He'd worked hard in the first period. The score was 1–1 against the Wildcats, which was a good start. He'd given Jake and his teammates all they could handle, scoring the goal off a sweet pass from Zachary for an easy one-timer from the slot.

Things had been sweet since Hilton took over as coach. Unburdened from coaching duties, Charlie had gone on a tremendous tear, scoring at a two-goal-a-game clip. It helped that Hilton had reunited him with Pudge and Zachary. All three had been scoring regularly. With only seven games left, a playoff spot secured and a good chance to finish third in the regular season, not to mention having recently tied a game with the mighty Snow Birds, Charlie had every reason to be stoked about the Rebels.

Hilton interrupted his thoughts.

"A good start," he said. "We took the body, skated well, and played smart in our own end. Frankly, I'm surprised how passive they've been. I can see their coach is having a word with his players. I can only imagine they'll be coming out guns blazing this period, so be on your toes." He looked at his clipboard. "Charlie's line is out."

Charlie went to centre. Schultz was really laying into his players. He could hear him yelling.

"That was the biggest piece of garbage period I've ever seen," he said. "I'm embarrassed. I didn't see a hit — not a single hit. You're letting them humiliate you — and me! Where's the toughness? Where's the commitment? Guys will be sitting on the bench very shortly if that doesn't change — and I mean immediately."

He lowered his voice and Charlie couldn't hear. A few Wildcats turned to look at him, which kind of weirded him out, like they were talking about him. Jake continued to stare after most had turned away. He had no time for Jake's tough-guy act. He skated over to Pudge.

"Too bad *he's* not our coach," he said.

"I played for him for two years and trust me, this is nothing. He's being nice. Wait till he gets worked up about something. It's a whole other level of insane."

"Can't believe anyone would play with him," Zachary said. "We've got to win this game. I can't even think about losing to this crew."

"Only possibility is victory," Pudge said.

The referee skated to the circle. Jake came out for the draw. Jake was all business as he lined up. Charlie took a moment to check out his stance — shoulders square, well balanced, feet slightly wider than shoulder width. Hard to know what Jake was thinking. He decided to go forehand and send it over to Zachary. He and Jake leaned forward in anticipation, their helmets touching slightly. The puck dropped. Quick as a flash,

Charlie slapped the puck to Zachary, following through with a shoulder. Zachary had timed it perfectly and picked up the puck on the fly, barrelling down the wing. Charlie sidestepped Jake and took off after him. After two strides he felt a sharp pain in his ribs — courtesy of a Jake butt-end.

"Out of my way, loser," Jake said.

He couldn't let Jake get away with that. He cut in front of him, and thrust his elbow into Jake's chin.

"Enjoy," he said, skating off.

Luckily the ref hadn't seen it. Roscoe came over to cover him. Charlie pretended to slow down, and then turned on the jets and blew by. Roscoe slapped his stick in frustration.

Zachary had taken it to the outside. The left defenceman cut him off, so he hit the brakes at the hash marks looking to pass. Charlie powered into the zone pointing to the corner. Zachary waited until he was in the slot and slid the puck down low.

Charlie glanced to his left. The other defenceman was covering the front of the net. Jake and Roscoe were somewhere behind him — probably not by much. Out of the corner of his eye he saw Pudge hanging wide near the boards. That was Pudge — always thinking ahead. Charlie backhanded the puck behind the net along the boards to Pudge, and prepared himself for a hit. He knew Roscoe would be coming hard. Sure enough, the right winger launched himself. Charlie jumped to his right at the last second. Roscoe barely grazed his shoulder, and slammed into the boards.

"Was that supposed to hurt?" he said to Roscoe, and headed to the front of the net.

Something struck him hard on the side of his head, the force of the blow sending him skidding to the boards. He felt strange, as if he was floating on a cloud.

"Maybe that'll hurt."

Charlie had trouble focusing. He knew that voice. Who was it?

Jake's leering face came into view. "You're out of your league, Joyce. We play for keeps." He shoved a glove into his face.

A ref pulled Jake aside, allowing Charlie to regain his feet. Pudge and Zachary raced in.

"That was the cheapest shot I've ever seen," Pudge thundered. Charlie had never seen Pudge so mad.

"Go eat a doughnut," Jake snarled, and he pushed forward to get at Pudge.

Liam and Roscoe crowded close, and Scott and Nick joined the scrum.

"Can't take a hit," Liam taunted.

"Maybe Joyce needs a diaper change," Thomas added.

"Maybe you guys need to repeat grade three again," Scott replied.

Charlie was having trouble concentrating. He moved away to give himself a chance to clear his head.

Tweet! Tweet! Tweet! Tweet!

Both referees were blowing their whistles non-stop. Charlie barely heard them, the crowd was making so much noise.

One spectator lifted himself over the top of the glass. "Call a penalty once in a while, ref," he bellowed. "You made this happen with your stupid calls."

A group of Wildcats supporters began chanting,

"Rebels suck! Rebels suck! Rebels suck!"

The referees began forcing the players to their respective benches, their whistles blasting away. Charlie was more than willing to follow. He needed to sit. His legs were tired, and he really needed a drink of water.

"Time to finish the job, prissy boy."

He felt a glove punch him in the mask. He knew it was Jake — he just couldn't see his face very clearly.

"You're goin' down, loser. It's punishment time," Jake snarled.

Charlie blinked rapidly to clear his head, but everything was still blurry. What was wrong with him?

Jake cuffed him on the side of his helmet. Charlie scrunched his eyes tightly and then opened them. For a moment he saw Jake clearly. He had his tough guy face on — eyes narrowed, a cocky grin, nodding slightly. He'd seen that face way too often. Charlie motioned Jake towards him with his glove. Maybe this was for the best. Settle it once and for all.

Jack threw a wild right cross without warning. Charlie ducked and drifted to his right. The sudden move made him feel sick to his stomach. He ignored it and fired a left jab. It connected, but not hard enough to slow Jake down. He answered with a series of left jabs to his face. Charlie backed up, trying to get some distance. Jack kept at him.

Charlie was scared. He'd fought before. This time something had sapped his energy. His legs were dead and he could barely hold his arms up. He tried to block Jake's blows, but it was as if he had ten fists. Jake connected with several good shots to his head. Charlie bent low and held his right arm in front of his face, and peered underneath. Jake took off his right glove. Why would he do that? Charlie wondered. I'm wearing a cage.

Jake feinted with a left jab, and then brought a vicious right hook to his ribs. Charlie couldn't move. The blow took his breath away. He struggled to stay on his feet. Without thinking he lowered his guard. A ref grabbed at Jake's sweater, but before he could pull him away, Jake threw a final right hook into his jaw. All the strength in Charlie's legs disappeared. He fell.

Jake raised both arms over his head as the ref dragged him away.

Charlie heard the crowd roar. The Wildcats banged their sticks on the boards. He really felt sick to his stomach. His ribs killed, and his head throbbed. The humiliation hurt far more, however. Jake had bashed him around like a little kid, in front of everyone. How pathetic. Great captain! He'd never live this down — never.

"Hey, Charlie. You okay?"

He couldn't make out the face. "What?"

"Let me help you up. You sure you're okay?"

It was Pudge. This was totally embarrassing. Julia was in the crowd and he was being helped like a baby.

Martin peered into his face. "Get up slow. You took some tough shots. Take it easy."

"Let's get him to the bench," Pudge said.

Pudge and Martin tried to slip their arms under his. Charlie pulled away.

"I'm cool. I'm not five years old. I can skate."

He headed to the bench, only to have Pudge spin him around.

"Let go," Charlie yelled.

"That's not our bench," Pudge whispered.

Unfortunately, the Wildcats noticed his mistake.

"You wanna come play for us now?" Jake called out. He was sitting on top of the boards. "You could be our team punching bag."

He was the all-time loser. How could he go to the wrong bench?

"That's your best idea yet," Liam said, trading a high-five with Jake. "Maybe he could double as our team soccer ball too.

"I think the little boy is scared," Roscoe said. "Don't be mean."

He tried to respond. For some reason the words wouldn't come.

Scott came to his rescue. "Hey Roscoe. I forgot to congratulate you on being voted the biggest doofus in school. Well done."

"Don't forget Jake got the bed-wetting award," Nick added.

The Wildcats' coach stepped down from the bench. He leaned over the boards and pointed at them.

"Take your pretty pink sweaters and get into house league. Triple-A ain't for the likes of you. I don't know what the league was thinking when they let you set up this joke of a team. I'm tempted to come onto the ice and teach you all a lesson you won't soon forget."

Charlie felt someone brush past his shoulder. Hilton walked towards Schultz. The entire rink went dead quiet; even the referees watched the drama unfold. Hilton continued his approach until he was almost nose to nose with the Wildcats' coach.

"I appreciate that this game got out of control," Hilton said. "Maybe you think my players started it. Obviously, I don't agree."

"Joyce was cheap-shotting me all game," Jake interjected.

Hilton ignored him. "Regardless of why this began, there is no excuse for you to try to intimidate my players. You're the adult here. That was the first and last time you'll ever threaten my boys. Understood?" Hilton kept his gaze fixed on Schultz.

Schultz shrugged and stepped down. "I've been coaching for twenty years. I don't have to tolerate this garbage, and I certainly don't have to listen to you." And with that he turned his back on the Rebels coach.

"Can you make it back to our bench yourself?" Hilton asked Charlie in a low voice.

He wasn't too sure at this point. "I don't know," he murmured.

Pudge slipped his arm under his and guided him over.

Jake leaned over the boards. "Joyce, don't go. I wanna hit you one more time — it was that much fun."

Charlie's head was still pounding as he sat on the bench, and he felt completely exhausted, as if he'd played ten games back to back.

"What period is it?" he asked Pudge.

Pudge looked at him strangely. "Hey, Jeffrey," he called out. "I think Charlie's really hurt."

His teammates crowded around.

"I'm good. I'm good," Charlie said. "I just need some water."

"How many fingers am I holding up?" Pudge asked.

He looked at Pudge's hand. He was going to say one, and then thought it was two.

"Two," he guessed.

"You think he got a concussion?" Zachary asked.

"I thought he was kinda dopey out there," Nick said.

"You saw Jake's cross-check," Pudge said. "He bashed him right below the ear. That explains why Charlie could barely fight."

"Only Jake would fight a guy with a concussion," Scott said. He took a swig of water and spit it onto the ice.

"Move aside, gentlemen," Hilton said.

Jeffrey pushed past the players, brought out a small flashlight from his medical kit, and flashed the light into Charlie's eyes. "Can you tell me how many fingers I'm holding up?" he said.

"Why is everyone asking me that?" Charlie replied.

"Does that mean you know?"

"Three, I think."

Jeffrey sighed. "We better get him to the hospital. He definitely has a concussion. Only question is what degree. He got hit hard by that kid's stick." Jeffrey turned Charlie's head slightly and peered closely at his ear.

"Your grandfather will have to take you," Hilton said.

"Is he here?" Charlie asked. He couldn't remember anything — the period, the score, or who they played. Sleep was the only think he could think about. He closed his eyes.

"No you don't," Jeffrey said. "First rule of concussions is you can't fall asleep."

Charlie felt some water run down his neck and splash on his cheeks. It was cold, but he didn't have the energy to protest.

"Jeffrey, help him into the dressing room and get his equipment off," Hilton ordered. "Give me a call when you know how he is," he said to Charlie's grandfather.

A floating feeling took over as Charlie felt himself lifted from the bench. He wondered where he was.

"When does the game start?" he blurted.

23

BLAH, BLAH

"I'll see you soon, Mom," Charlie called out from the hallway.

"You're still here? I thought you'd left already."

"I guess . . . I . . . lost track of time."

"I'm glad you finally decided to go. You shouldn't miss your dance. It sounds like a lot of fun, and your friends will be glad to see you after three weeks at home."

He hadn't been back to school since the concussion, and he wasn't that stoked about this dance. He knew Jake and his crew would give him a hard time about the fight, and his friends . . . well, they would be all embarrassed. If it were up to him, he'd stay home and watch TV. But his mom had been bugging him so much to go that he finally gave in.

"I'll see you soon, Mom. I probably won't stay too long."

"Okay, dear." She pointed at his feet. "Could you at least put on some boots? It's supposed to continue snowing all night."

His reputation was bad enough without looking like a doofus in snow boots.

"It's like two minutes to school. I'm good. See ya."

"Charlie!"

He headed off to school. For a week after the game he'd had a bad headache and felt dizzy a lot of the time. His head felt better now. It couldn't be that bad to talk to a few people, then leave. As he walked along he had to admit it felt good to be outside. He never thought he could get bored with TV and video games.

His mom had been right about one thing — it was snowing hard. He picked up the pace, but the bottoms of his pants were soaked and he could barely feel his toes by the time he got to school. He could hear the music blaring as he slowly pushed open the gym doors. It hit him like a wall of sound. He'd been particularly sensitive to noise since the concussion. He forced himself to ignore it and went inside. He couldn't ignore the butterflies in his stomach, however. Why did that always happen? It was only a dumb dance, and he wasn't going to stay long.

A huge banner at the far end of the gym proclaimed: *The 23rd Annual Beat the Winter Blahs Dance – Kick It!* The DJ was organizing a large group of kids into two lines. Snacks and soft drinks were set up against one wall. A handful of dancers were off to the side, a strobe light making it look as if they were moving in slow motion.

On the far side of the gym by the bleachers he saw Pudge, Nick and Zachary. He watched the dancers as he made his way over to his friends — which is why he didn't see Jake, Liam, Thomas and Roscoe next to the refreshments table. By the time he did, it was too late. Liam pointed him out.

"Joyce finally makes his big return," he said loudly.

"About time the little chicken came back," Jake mocked.

Roscoe laughed. "Be nice, Jake. You don't want to make him cry again. Look — too late. He's got tears in his eyes already."

Jake and Roscoe high-fived.

Charlie's heart pounded as he walked past. A few kids standing around laughed or turned to look the other way. He wanted to charge at Jake and wipe that look off his face.

His friends gave him a big cheer when they saw him. He punched fists all around and endured some good-natured cracks about his soft head. Pudge held out his fist and Charlie gave it a punch and sat down. Scott emerged from the middle of the dance floor, busting moves his whole way over, his forehead glittering with sweat.

"Dudes, it's worse than I thought. The ladies are fighting over me. The hip hop classes are totally paying off."

That set them howling.

"Where are your tutu and slippers?" Nick said.

"Laugh if you want — these magic feet are in high demand. You losers can blend into the walls and watch." He looked around. "Dance partner at six o'clock," he said, nodding toward the doors.

Alexandra was standing next to Rebecca. Scott danced his way over, winking to his friends as he did. Charlie had to hand it to him. He wasn't shy around girls — and he didn't care what other people thought. Charlie could probably learn something from him. He cheered along with the others as Scott led Alexandra to the dance floor.

Nick elbowed Charlie.

"The dude can dance, I'll give him that," he said. "Maybe a few lessons would help me. I don't want to spend the rest of my life watching every dance I go to."

"I hear ya," Charlie said. "I've never perfected my spins — not like Scott, anyway."

That wasn't entirely true. He'd never admit it to Nick, but when he was younger his mother had forced him to take dance lessons. He'd been pretty good at it too, but he stopped after a few years. In any case, he was too self-conscious to get out on the dance floor now.

Zachary tossed his cup into the garbage, basketball-style. "Can't let Scott get all the glory," he said.

The next thing, Zachary and Rebecca were dancing together.

Jonathon came by and sat next to Charlie. "How're the rest of the Rebels doing?" he said.

"Scott seems to be doing all right," Charlie said, "and Zachary's trying to keep up."

"That's cool," Jonathon said. "You been out there yet?"

He shrugged and shook his head. "Just got here. I'm gonna take it easy tonight. This music is tough for me to take right now."

"So how's the melon?" Jonathon said, tapping the top of his head.

"It's good. Doc said I should be able to come back for the last couple of games before the playoffs."

"I think it's a miracle you can play again at all. Jake should go to jail for that cross-check." Jonathon pointed to the other side of the gym. "Your buddy is in the house, by the way,"

"I saw him," Charlie replied grimly.

"Can't believe he got off with only a two-game suspension," Jonathon said.

"Should be out of the league," Pudge added.

"We'll play them again," Nick said darkly.

The talk about Jake embarrassed Charlie. He'd been totally schooled, and everyone knew it.

"Forget Jake," he said. "He's not worth it. We'll get ours back by winning the championship." He didn't really believe that. It just seemed the right thing to say.

Jonathon elbowed Charlie. "I see Julia," he said. "Want to go over with me and say hi?"

Charlie was all too conscious of the blood rushing to his cheeks. All the guys would be watching, and they'd bug him about it forever.

"You go ahead," he said. "I'll come over later."

Jonathon looked surprised. "Cool, dude. I'll tell her." He got up. "You should ask her to dance," he said before he left.

Charlie watched Jonathon sneak up and pull her ponytail. She whirled around, and when she saw it was Jonathon, promptly punched him in the arm. Jonathon pretended to box for a second, and then they began to talk. Charlie felt silly. He wished he could talk to girls without making it into such a big deal.

The conversation quickly turned to hockey — as usual. Matt, Pudge and Dylan discussed the Rebels' playoff chances. Since the Wildcats game, things had gone off the rails. Without Charlie's offence, goals became scarce, and they were down to nine players.

194

They'd lost five in a row, and with just three games left they'd blown their chance at third. Fortunately, their earlier hot streak ensured fourth place, and a first-round game against the Hornets.

He sat quietly off to the side. No one paid him much notice. After the concussion, his teammates had come to see him at home, but their visits only made him feel worse. He could sense they only came to be nice. He'd lost their respect. How could they respect him after he totally choked against Jake? He'd made the entire team look bad. It didn't help that he'd been completely bossy at the start of the season, trying to be coach and captain. He'd yelled at the guys and acted liked he owned the team. Even sitting around like this was embarrassing for him, and he began to wish he hadn't let his mom talk him into coming.

As he was thinking about when he could leave without attracting too much attention, two dancers caught his eye. At first he couldn't believe it. His heart started pounding, and he felt slightly queasy. It confirmed everything he'd been thinking. Julia was dancing with Jake! So Jonathon had been messing with him after all. Charlie would ask her to dance and she would laugh in his face. Julia wanted to dance with the coolest guy in school — and the guy who'd pummeled Charlie Joyce. Deep down, he'd always known Julia liked Jake.

He wasn't going to watch them dance. He got up and started walking towards the doors. Even the thought of leaving made him feel better. In ten minutes he'd be home. As he reached the stairs he heard his named called.

"Charlie, what's up?" Pudge was hurrying over.

"You were sitting there by yourself and then took off all of a sudden. Is everything okay?"

"I'm going home, I think. I might have pushed things a bit. I've got a headache and my neck's killing me. I'm tired and . . . I'm just gonna go."

"I'll call my dad and he can give us a lift. You shouldn't walk home, not with the storm. I've got my cell. I'll give him a call."

"I'm fine. I'll walk. The music is too loud, that's all. Fresh air will be good."

"Fresh air? It's snowing like crazy."

"I got here okay."

"Wait two minutes and my dad . . ."

"I'm not your baby brother. I walk home from school every day. I'm not going to die."

Pudge's shoulder's stiffened. He shrugged, and crossed his arms.

"Whatever."

Pudge's feelings were obviously hurt. Was it wrong to want to go home? It's not like anyone would miss him.

"I'll see you . . . later."

Pudge barely nodded.

"See you later," he repeated.

Pudge shrugged again.

He couldn't stand Pudge being angry with him. Maybe he took Pudge for granted sometimes.

Charlie cleared his throat. "Sorry, dude. I was . . . that was . . . it's the headache. This concussion's messed me up. I'm tired and I say . . . stupid stuff. Anyway, you're right. I'm being dumb." He leaned closer and said quietly, "I didn't want to look like a loser, so I wore my running shoes. My feet are swimming in water." Pudge laughed and Charlie felt better. "Call your dad. That's a good idea. That is, if you don't mind leaving so early."

Pudge waved his cell phone. "I've watched other people dance long enough. I'll call from the hallway where it's quieter."

Pudge left. Charlie looked out over the dance floor. Scott was still dancing with Alexandra. He didn't see Zachary or Jonathon — or Jake. He felt something jab him hard in the back. He was willing to bet it was Jake messing with him. He spun around.

"Where are you going?" Julia asked. She folded her arms. "I haven't seen you on the dance floor yet."

Well, he'd certainly seen her.

Charlie looked away. "I'm not the biggest dancer around," he mumbled.

Julia giggled.

He shook his head. "I mean, I'm not so into dancing. I was hanging with the boys . . . the Rebels . . . teammates . . . from my hockey team."

Julia put her hand on Charlie's arm. "How are you feeling?" she asked. "I was worried when you missed all that school."

Her concern came as a surprise to him. "The doctor said I can maybe come back to school next week," he answered. "But probably no hockey or anything like that for at least one more week." He tapped his head. "Concussion."

Charlie felt himself blush. That sounded lame.

"I couldn't believe what happened." She tucked her hair behind her ears. "Jake went way too far. I don't understand him. He used to be a really nice guy — lately all he cares about is showing off and trying to be Mr. Cool."

Was she talking about Jake — a really nice guy? Without thinking, he shot back, "Why don't you ask him about it when you dance together again?"

Her shoulders sagged and she brushed her hair aside. "That was nothing. A bunch of us were dancing and he . . ." She raised her eyebrows. "We've been to the same school since, like, grade one . . . and I thought it would be a bit rude to say no because he asked in a nice way and . . . It was only for one dance."

His mouth had gone dry. He swallowed, but it didn't seem to help.

He shrugged. "It's your life. None of my business."

He wished he could have taken that back because her eyes narrowed and her cheeks grew flushed. Now he'd insulted her. First Pudge, now Julia. He put his hands on the railing and leaned back. He needed to tell her how he felt. Then he could leave with Pudge and it would be over.

"To be honest, maybe I was bummed out a bit when I saw you dancing with Jake." He crossed his arms. "I know I'm being pathetic. You probably don't know, but Jake and I — we kind of have this . . . I guess you'd call it a rivalry." He sighed deeply. "He's hated me since the first day at school. Maybe he doesn't like the way I look — who knows?" He swallowed again, but nothing seemed to help. His throat was like a desert. "Maybe also I'm a little embarrassed by what happened."

"What do you mean? Why would you be embarrassed?"

198

"You saw it — the fight." He lowered his eyes to the floor. "I really let the guys down. I was almost glad I got the concussion, so I didn't have to come to school the next day. I can just imagine what Jake, Liam and all the guys said about me."

"They talk a lot, for sure." She looked up at him. "Besides, I don't think fighting is all that impressive . . . and I don't think you're being pathetic either."

Charlie was dying for a glass of water. His palms were wet too. What was going on? On top of everything, he was getting sick now? He'd been stupid to walk in the snow.

She scrunched her mouth to one side. "So are you having fun at the dance, Charlie?"

The question caught him off guard. He hadn't enjoyed it at all, but he wasn't sure he should say that to Julia.

"It's okay, I guess. Like I said, I'm not much one for dances."

She looked disappointed. "Your friend Scott certainly likes to dance. Poor Alex can't get off the floor."

"I think that's part of his plan," he said.

She arched her eyebrows. "He's a nice guy. I think Alex likes him."

"I think he likes her too."

"Hmm — ya think?"

He laughed. "Scott's not the shy type."

"At least you know what he's thinking," she said.

Was that a dig at me? he wondered. Julia looked up at him, but didn't say anything more. She was obviously waiting for him to talk. Why was it so easy to talk to his friends and so hard to talk to Julia?

The silence was becoming awkward. He had to say something. Out of the corner of his eye, he spotted Jake. He had a drink in his hand, and was staring right at him. That decided it. Stop acting like such a wimp, Joyce! he said to himself.

"So you were saying it's rude for a girl not to dance," he said, feeling his face grow hot.

"What do you mean?"

This was torture. Just say it!

"Well, didn't you say that?" he said weakly.

"I said I thought it would be rude to say no to Jake considering he asked nicely and I've known him since primary school . . ."

She smiled. He gathered his courage.

"So . . . um . . . you wanna . . . ?"

The door opened and Pudge's head popped in.

"There you are," he said. "My dad's gonna be here in a minute. He told us to wait by the front doors." He looked over at Julia. "Oh, hi, Julia. Didn't see you. How's it going?"

"It's good, Pudge."

"Let's go, Charlie," Pudge said.

Julia looked over at Charlie.

What a spot to be in. He was dying to hang out with Julia, but he couldn't tell Pudge he didn't want to leave now.

"Sorry, Julia. I have to go. Pudge's dad is giving us a lift home."

"But the dance has just gotten started," she said.

"I know, but my head's starting to hurt . . . The music is getting to me, I guess."

Julia pouted. "Okay. If you're not feeling well, you

should . . . I suppose it makes sense that you go. You don't want to make it worse."

"See ya," he said.

"See ya," she replied. "And you too, Pudge."

He watched her skip down the stairs, and then he followed Pudge to the front of the school. How was that for bad timing? Maybe it was for the best. She was probably only pretending to be nice, anyway. She'd dance with Jake again — he knew it.

"So what were you talking to Julia about?" Pudge asked.

"Nothing — school stuff, the essay for Hilton."

Pudge looked out the window towards the street. "There he is," he said. "Come on."

"Are there other dances this year — school dances, I mean?" Charlie asked, as they ran to the truck.

"I don't think so," Pudge said. "The grade twelves have a prom dance at the end of the year."

Charlie clambered in. He was grateful for the warmth. The storm was really picking up. He sat back, tired and listless. What a mess things were. No hockey; he was the laughingstock of the school, and an embarrassment to his teammates; and he'd blown his only chance to dance with Julia.

"So, how was the dance, boys?" Pudge's father asked.

"Good," Charlie said politely.

Nothing could have been further from the truth.

24

SNOW BALL

Charlie packed the snow between his mitts and fired it at the trunk of a large tree. Yet another storm had swept across Terrence Falls, dumping a foot of snow. Kids were going crazy playing in the huge snowdrifts. He tossed a few more snowballs at the tree to keep warm, looking over at the school every few throws and wishing the bell would ring. Lunch period was taking forever. In the distance he could hear some guys shouting. Pudge had told him about a snow soccer game. He'd taken a look, and left immediately when he saw Jake was there.

That's how it had been this last couple of weeks since he'd come back to school. He couldn't bring himself to face Jake — or anyone for that matter. He'd become the biggest joke in school. Everyone looked at him differently. They all knew about the fight, how Jake had humiliated him. As for Julia, she hadn't said a word to him since the dance.

Hockey had always been the one thing in his life he could count on, but not lately. The fun had gone out of the game. The Rebels lost the last three games of the regular season, and he'd played terribly in the last two, barely getting a shot on net. After the final game,

Charlie had asked Hilton to take the captaincy away from him. What good was a captain who let his team-mates down? Hilton had refused. He said the team had voted him captain, and they would win or lose with him as captain.

As expected, the Snow Birds and the Wildcats finished one-two respectively and had earned first-round byes in the playoffs. The Rebels' first playoff game was tonight against the Hornets, and the winner would play the mighty Snow Birds. Mike Dunn had been bragging the past few days that the Hornets were going to destroy them. Scott and some of the others had traded some trash talk. He'd kept out of it.

Charlie was thinking about the playoffs when he felt something smack into his back. He turned. Pudge held a snowball and was winding up for another throw. Charlie dodged it, scooped up a snowball, and rifled it into Pudge's stomach. Pudge laughed and jogged over.

"Where have you been?" Pudge asked. "I thought you were going to play soccer. It was pretty funny. Scott tripped over the ball and slid face first into a snowdrift — although being Scott, it was probably on purpose." Pudge brushed some snow off his sleeve. "Is this snow crazy or what?"

"I was going to come over, but remembered I had some homework . . . science and math. I went to the library." He felt bad lying to Pudge, but he could hardly tell him he was afraid to play soccer against Jake.

Pudge frowned. "You've been at the library three times this week, and you went last week too."

"My mom read me the riot act about school work. I've been trying to raise my marks."

He looked at the school again, as if he could will the bell to ring.

Pudge folded his arms. "A little snow soccer isn't going to kill you."

"Maybe tomorrow."

"You say that all the time — and you always have an excuse. What about Saturday? We all came to school for football — Scott, Nick, Me, Zachary, Matt — and you didn't show. We only had five guys, which made it kind of tough to make two teams."

"I told you I had to finish that geography presentation."

"We all did. But you said you'd be there."

That was true, but at the last minute he'd changed his mind. How could he explain it? Nothing was the same after the fight, not with school, not with the team — not even with Pudge.

"You've even missed two practices in a row," Pudge continued.

"I've been busy at school, and at my mom's café."

Pudge took a deep breath. "Charlie, some of the guys have been talking. They kind of voted me . . . like the spokesman." He paused before continuing. "What's going on with you? It's like you don't want to do anything anymore . . . like hang out . . . or even play hockey."

"That's whacked, dude."

"Then explain why you've disappeared," Pudge said heatedly. "Where's the guy who's all over the ice, going end to end and scoring. You're going through the motions, and everyone's wondering why. Last game you barely touched the puck. You were second in scoring in the league and since you've come back I don't think you've had a point."

"In case you didn't notice, I had a concussion. It's not so easy to just come back and score a ton of goals. I'm the first to admit I'm in a scoring slump. That's obvious. It's not like I don't want to score." He scooped up some snow and squished it into a ball.

"It's not just that," Pudge said. "You're not playing . . . like before." He looked off towards the road. "Straight out, there's no effort, Charlie. You're soft on the puck. No one used to be able to take the puck off you — now everyone does. When you get some open ice, you pass. It's like . . . you lost all your confidence or something."

"I'm trying!" Charlie shouted. He slapped his thigh with his fist. "I knew guys were dissing me. I knew it. You all think I don't hear. You think I'm so stupid that I don't get it." He felt completely betrayed. Everyone had turned on him. "I practically got killed playing for you guys. I put the stupid Rebels together and . . . and . . . now you want me off the team!" He wanted to run home then and there and never come back.

"I never said that," Pudge said. "Guys want to know what's wrong. It's like you're mad at us, and we didn't do anything. No one understands what happened. You barely talk anymore. You don't even want to be friends with us . . ."

"Tell the Rebels I'll quit, which is what everyone wants."

"It is not!" Pudge thundered. "No one wants you to quit. We want Charlie Joyce to be Charlie Joyce — the guy we voted captain." He pointed a glove at

Charlie. "We have a playoff game tonight and you wanna quit! Act like the captain, and not some guy who feels sorry for himself — and is afraid to play snow soccer."

"That's dumb."

"I don't think so. What's dumb is quitting on the team and your friends because of one game — one fight. Why do you care so much? It's over. You're the only one who doesn't get it. I don't know who's acting like the bigger jerk, you or Jake."

With that, turned and left. Charlie watched without moving, still holding the snowball. He didn't have a friend left in school. Everything he'd tried to do with the Rebels had been a waste.

It was better back when he didn't know anyone at school. He'd never felt so lonely since he'd arrived at Terrence Falls. He'd never fit in here — never.

* * *

Hours later, Charlie sat in the dressing room tying his skates, a knot in his stomach getting worse as game time approached. He'd changed his mind half a dozen times. He'd finally decided not to play — he could simply blame the concussion — but then his mom yelled that she was ready to go to the game, and his sister and grandparents were waiting in the van. That left him no choice, and so he came, dreading every minute.

A slap on the shin pads interrupted his thoughts.

"Is the Joyce-monster ready to roll?" Scott said.

He felt scared more than ready. He nodded weakly.

"This is your game, dude." Scott whacked him on the pads again. "No one's got your wheels. Get to the puck and go."

The praise embarrassed him. "Big game, for sure."

He couldn't think of anything else to say.

"Their defence pinches," Zachary said to Charlie from across the room. "I'll be chippin' the puck off the boards to you all game. You'll get a ton of breakaways."

"We gotta get our power play going," Pudge said. "It was awesome early in the season. Get the puck to Charlie and let him attack the zone. Me and Zachary will charge the net."

There was a brief silence

"First goal will be huge," Matt interjected. He bounced his stick a few times on the floor. "You ready for this one, Char?"

"I guess," he said.

He caught Matt exchanging a glance with Zachary. He grabbed his helmet and sat up. Only then did he notice that all his teammates were all looking at him. Had he forgotten something? He quickly checked his equipment. What was going on?

"So, captain . . . what do you think . . . about the Hornets?" Pudge asked.

All of a sudden it dawned on him that his teammates were trying to restore his confidence and get him stoked for the game. He looked at the serious faces around him. Even Scott was quiet. Most games the guys were laughing and joking — now, you could hear a pin drop. There was no question the boys wanted this game. Charlie tossed his helmet a few times. He realized that Pudge had been right. His teammates hadn't quit on him — he'd quit on his teammates. He'd let Jake totally intimidate him; he'd let him destroy his confidence. The concussion had been a convenient excuse for being a wuss. Charlie thought about what his dad had always said to him after he'd had a bad game. "I don't worry about you winning or losing; I just want to see you trying to help your team win." The memory of his father made him feel ashamed. It was as if he'd let his dad down.

Pudge had just called him captain — time to prove he deserved the C.

"I don't think anything about the Hornets," he began. "This game isn't about the Hornets. It's about the Rebels. We've got enough talent to beat anyone when we play our game. We proved that in the regular season. Maybe we haven't played too great lately — and that goes double for me. But that was then. The Hornets aren't in our league — no chance."

No one spoke. They all kept looking at him. He had to keep going until Hilton came in.

"I could think of a lot of reasons to get stoked for this game. It's the playoffs. It's sudden-death. We got up at five in the morning to practise in the middle of winter. We didn't even have a coach until Christmas."

His teammates were all nodding. He was on the right track. He flipped his helmet around and sat up straight.

"But that's not why I want to win this game."

His gaze settled on Pudge.

"So what's the reason?" Pudge asked.

"I want to shut Mike Dunn up for good, and his dad too."

That did it. Everyone began to talk at once.

"We've got to win every battle along the walls," said Christopher, taking Charlie by surprise. He rarely spoke in the dressing room.

"Hard on every puck — every loose puck is ours." Now Robert was getting into it.

We'll take these pretenders out by the end of the first," Scott added.

"Clear the front of the net for Martin and we got ourselves a shutout," Nick said.

"These dudes got nothin'. It's our game all the way," Zachary said.

"We can outskate the Hornets backwards and forwards," Jonathon added. "Fire on all cylinders, boys."

Charlie's heart was pounding.

The door opened and Hilton came in. He looked around and then smiled at Charlie.

"You started this team — only you can keep it going. I assume whatever needed to be said has been said."

Charlie jumped to his feet. "Remember why we want to win this game, and there's no way we can lose."

He led his teammates onto the ice.

MIKE PSYCH

The Hornets' right winger flipped the puck to the right corner. Charlie raced after it, with Mike Dunn a step behind.

"Out of my way, Joyce!" Mike yelled.

Charlie had to act fast. The puck lay against the boards. He extended his stick and drew the puck between his skates. Leaping to his right he did a three-sixty spin to avoid the collision.

Boom!

Mike crashed into the boards and fell to the ice. Charlie had no time to enjoy the sight as another Hornets forechecker bore down on him. Across the zone, Scott raised his stick and whistled. He was wide open. Charlie was about to pass when he heard a girl's voice ring out from the crowd.

"Go for it, Charlie!"

That sounded like Julia. Whoever it was, he decided to follow the advice. Feinting to his left and then pivoting on his right foot, he pirouetted around the surprised forechecker. The roar of the crowd fired him up as he raced up ice. He felt his confidence soar as he picked up speed in the neutral zone.

Zachary cut across the blue line from the right wing. Since his return from the concussion, Charlie had been passing in this situation, treating the puck like a hot potato. This time, he was determined to go for it himself. He faked the pass and let Zachary cut underneath, angling to the right. Five feet from the defenceman, he pretended to lose the puck in his skates. The defenceman fell for it and charged. Charlie instantly kicked the puck to his stick, dipped his left shoulder to the inside, and then popped to the outside.

Zachary and Pudge poured into the Hornets' zone. Three-on-one. The defenceman swung his stick frantically back and forth. Charlie carried the puck to the top of the circle. Zachary had slowed, his stick over his head, ready for the one-timer, while Pudge pushed on towards the net.

Charlie bent his right knee and turned sideways, dragging the puck behind him as if to pass to Zachary. The defenceman dropped to one knee and swung his stick in a wide arc to block the pass. But Charlie had meanwhile pulled the puck across to his backhand and was able to slip past him.

Charlie closed in on the goalie. Pudge had parked himself on the edge of the crease. Eight feet out, he swung his stick as if to backhand it to Pudge. The goalie threw his right pad down in anticipation. But the puck was still on Charlie's stick. The goalie had the presence of mind to reach his left leg out, almost doing the splits. Charlie swung the puck to this forehand and cut hard across the top of the crease. In one motion, he jammed the puck between the goalie's legs before crashing head-long into Pudge.

Charlie sprung back to his feet. He was so stoked he wanted to race back to centre for the faceoff. Pudge held out his glove and Charlie gave it a hard punch.

"If I'd known you had it covered I would've saved my energy and watched," Pudge said, grinning widely.

"Your goal, bud," Charlie said. He cuffed the back of Pudge's helmet. "Goalie had to cover you and that left the five-hole open."

"You're right," Pudge laughed. "That was all me."

Zachary draped his arms across their shoulders. "First-goal fever. I want three more before the period ends."

Nick and Scott arrived next, and they pounded his helmet so many times he said, "Easy, boys. I've had enough concussions for one season."

They drifted back to their end. The Rebels supporters were on their feet, cheering wildly. He spotted Danielle swinging her cowbell and holding a bag of popcorn in her other hand. His mom and grandparents clapped along with the other parents. Further down in the stands some kids from school were going crazy. Julia, Alexandra and Rebecca were in the middle clapping as they chanted, "*Re-bels! Re-bels! Re-bels!*"

Matt's line remained seated on the bench, and Charlie hurried to the faceoff circle before his coach decided to change the lines. Mike was already set up.

"Drop the puck, ref," Mike snarled. "They score one goal, and you'd think they'd won the championship."

The referee blew his whistle and held the puck over centre. When he let it drop, Mike swung his stick wildly, but Charlie blocked it, and then drew the puck to Scott. Mike bulled past and charged at Scott, who waited calmly until Mike had committed and then slid the puck between Mike's skates to Charlie. Charlie immediately whirled around and headed towards the Hornets' goal. Zachary cut across the blue line and this time Charlie passed to him. Zachary danced around the right winger and curled into the Hornets' end along the wall. Charlie followed behind.

"Zachary, drop it," he called.

Zachary left the puck for him and set up in the corner. Pudge charged the net, as usual. Charlie was tempted to blast one from the top of the circle, but opted to slide the puck to Zachary down low. The right defenceman moved to pressure the puck, which left the area to the goalie's right wide open. Zachary lifted the puck to that spot — and Charlie extended full out to corral it. The defenceman covering Pudge threw himself to the ice to block his shot. Charlie took a step to reach around the prone player and managed to fling it to the front of the net to Pudge. He faked a shot, which made the goalie drop to a butterfly, and then passed it hard back to Charlie, who tilted his stick and redirected the puck just inside the right post.

During the entire play, Charlie hadn't heard a sound. But the second the puck went in the roar of the crowd washed over him, almost catching him off guard. Zachary held him in a bear hug and lifted him off the ice a few times. Pudge pounded his helmet and soon Scott and Nick were doing the same.

Charlie was too overwhelmed to say a word. He hadn't scored in what seemed like ages. All the pressure he'd put on himself was gone. That last goal had been all instinct. He didn't even have to think. His body had just reacted to the situation.

This time he headed to the bench, figuring Hilton would change it up. Matt, Jonathon and Dylan were bashing their sticks on the boards. Hilton nodded to centre. Charlie felt a surge of energy. Two goals on one shift — and a chance for a third!

Charlie lined up for the draw. The Hornets coach had his arm around Mike's neck, and he was talking, his right hand jabbing into the air forcefully. Then Mike skated over to centre. Just as Hilton was doing for him, the Hornets coach was giving Mike a chance to redeem himself. Charlie was determined to prove that was a mistake.

Mike changed his stance this time, widening his legs and holding his stick in a reverse grip. Charlie decided to try something unexpected. He also reversed his grip. But instead of pulling it back, he pushed the puck forward. Mike's wide stance made it impossible for him to slow Charlie up, and Charlie easily evaded his desperate hip check and surged forward with the puck.

He'd also surprised his linemates. They were still at the red line as he moved in on the defence. Since it was a one-on-two, he raised his stick to slap it in deep. The left defenceman turned to get a jump on the forecheck. That changed Charlie's mind. He kept the puck and skated right behind the defenceman, shoving the puck into his skates. The defenceman kept turning his head to find the puck, but Charlie kept it in his skates so he couldn't get at it. Finally, the defenceman spun to skate backwards. He was too slow, however. Charlie pulled the puck from his skates and slipped past his right shoulder.

The other defenceman stormed over to cut Charlie off. Charlie slid his right hand halfway down the shaft of his stick and used his left arm to fend off his opponent. The two players pushed against each other, Charlie struggling to cut to the net and the defenceman trying just as hard to stop him.

At the hash marks, Charlie realized he was running out of space. The goalie was way out to cut down the angle. A backhand was useless. He had to get to the slot. He slid the puck behind the defenceman's back and slipped back inside. The Hornets player gasped as Charlie gathered the puck alone in front. The goalie butterflied, but Charlie wasn't paying him much attention. He felt he could shoot through a brick wall. He reared back, hesitated slightly to put the goalie off, and let it fly. The puck nicked the right post and ricocheted in.

He thrust his arms over his head and pumped his arms. The captain was supposed to come through in big games. Well, he had — three goals in one shift!

After that, the rout was on. Before the first period ended, Matt scored another marker. By the end of the second it was 7–0. The Rebels supporters were chanting non-stop. Five minutes into the third, Dylan powered in from the wing and beat the goalie with a wicked shot on the short side. After that, the Rebels were content to kill the clock and the score ended 8–0.

Bhrrr.

The game was over! Martin threw his arms in the air. Scott and Nick jumped at him, and they went down in a heap, their delirious teammates following. Charlie didn't know quite how to feel. He'd never been so relieved to win a game.

"You did it," Pudge said, arm around his shoulders.

"Four goals and one assist."

"We did it," Charlie said.

"Bring on the Snow Birds," Nick yelled.

"There's a surprise," Scott said, pointing to the far boards. "Mike's leaving before we shake hands. I thought he'd want to congratulate his old teammates."

"I'm sure he'll drop by the dressing room," Nick said.

"Very cool, dudes," Zachary said.

"The Snow Birds will wish they never took up the game," Matt added, pounding everyone's helmet for good measure.

"Come on, guys. Mike's gone, but the rest of them are waiting," Charlie said.

He led the Rebels to centre to shake hands. Mike's teammates proved to be good sports, wishing them luck in the semis. As he was skating off, he heard someone call his name.

"Hey, Charlie, Pudge. Awesome game."

It was their sponsor, Brent. They skated over.

"Thanks for coming out," Charlie said. "We appreciate the support."

"Are you kidding?" he said. "Can't remember enjoying a game more. You all played great — made The Hockey Shop proud."

"I thought you were changing the name," Charlie said.

"Nah," he said. "In the end I couldn't do it. Too much history."

"Why change the perfect name?" Charlie said.

"Like the Rebels," Brent said. "It says it all."

Charlie couldn't have agreed more.

26

UP THE MIDDLE

Charlie saw the puck squirt free and bounce towards the blue line. Burnett reached out with his stick, but before he could gain control Charlie swung his stick and chipped it out of the Rebels' zone and down the ice. That was close! With Dylan and Zachary in the box to start the third, the Snow Birds had been buzzing all around the net to get the go-ahead goal.

Burnett had hustled back and carried the puck up the right side. Charlie drifted over to force a pass. He didn't want the talented rushing defenceman to take it into their end. He'd already scored off a fancy feed from Savard in the slot. That had made it 2–1 for the Snow Birds. Charlie tied it up at the end of the second, tipping Scott's blast from the point under Alexi's pad and into the left corner of the net.

Burnett fired the puck cross ice to his defence partner, who promptly flicked it to the speedy Savard. He bore down on Nick and Scott, took it outside, and then slammed on the brakes at the hash marks against the boards. His teammates flooded the zone, and the Rebels set up their triangle.

That gave Charlie a chance to survey the scene.

Burnett was inching into the slot. The left winger was down low in the corner, square to Savard. The right winger was at the far side of the net. He instantly recognized the formation. It was the Snow Birds' favourite play with the man advantage. Hilton had them practise against it all week. Savard would pass to his winger and shift to the top of the circle. Burnett charged the slot. The winger would look for Burnett first and, if covered, he'd pass back to Savard and go to the net.

Savard indeed passed to the winger down low. Charlie knew exactly what to do.

"I got the slot," he yelled, and took a few steps towards Burnett.

It was all deception. The winger assumed Charlie was going to cover Burnett, so he promptly passed to Savard without looking. Charlie had moved back to Savard, however. The puck went right to his stick. In one motion, Charlie whirled around and started up ice. Savard raced to get back on defence, which allowed Charlie to carry it out of his zone easily. He glanced quickly over his shoulder and noticed that the other Snow Birds, figuring he'd ice it, were backchecking very slowly.

He decided otherwise, cutting across the red line and then turning back to his own end. The move caught all the Snow Birds by surprise. He eluded the left winger and passed the puck to Nick. When Nick felt pressure from the other winger, he rifled it across to Scott at the far boards. The big defenceman cocked his stick, ready to slap it down the ice when a forechecker got near.

Charlie was thrilled. The Snow Birds were running around, and Zachary's penalty was almost over. He circled in his own end and called for it. Scott faked the shot and slid it over. Charlie sensed pressure coming from his left. He dipped his shoulder in that direction to force the player to commit, and then directed the puck the other way between his skates, spinning around at the same time. He heard Martin bang his stick on the ice to signal the end of the first penalty. He'd expended some energy and didn't think he had the legs for another rush, so after a few more strides he blasted the puck in deep.

"Change 'em up," he called.

Matt hopped the boards to take his place. On the bench, Charlie leaned his head against the boards, breathing heavily. He felt an arm across his back.

"Great positioning in our end," Hilton said.

He sat up. "Thanks, Coach. It happened just like in practice."

"But when you're the last man back," he continued, "could you please lay off the between-the-legs move. You almost gave me a heart attack."

"Sorry, Coach. I felt so confident. Maybe I got carried away."

He nodded. "Fair enough. How about we agree not to do it again — at least for this game."

"No problem."

Hilton slapped the top of his helmet and turned his attention back to the game.

"Awesome kill," Pudge said. "I don't know about you, but I'm feeling a momentum change."

"Me too. Remember, we tied these guys. They can be beaten." He stood up. "This is our game to win," he said to those on the bench. "They're getting frustrated.

The mistakes will happen, and we need to capitalize."

A roar from the crowd interrupted him. Matt had picked off an errant pass and was storming down the right side. Zachary came to the bench for a change, and Jonathon leapt over the boards to kill off the last thirty-five seconds of Dylan's penalty.

Charlie was too excited to sit and he cheered Matt and Jonathon on as they did a great job plugging the neutral zone. As Dylan jumped back on the ice, Charlie felt a hand on his shoulder.

"I want you three to be ready," Hilton said. "Savard and Burnett played that entire power play. They'll have to rest. Here's your chance to get out there and score."

"We're on it, Coach," Charlie said.

Charlie nudged Zachary's arm.

"Cheap penalty, bro," he said.

Zachary scowled. "Refs are blind. My stick hit the puck. He took a total dive."

"No harm done," Charlie said.

Matt was heading to the bench, his arm held high.

"Bombs away," Charlie said to his linemates as he hopped the boards.

Pudge and Zachary shifted on soon after. Christopher forced a bad pass in the neutral zone with a solid hit against the boards. His brother swooped in and passed to Zachary in one motion. He cut inside, blowing by the centre who'd tried to hold him up with his stick. Zachary was still angry about the penalty, and no stick check was going to slow him down. Meanwhile, Charlie was tearing along the right wall.

Just before he crossed the blue line, Zachary flipped him a cross-ice pass. Charlie took it in full flight, beating the defender outside and cutting in sharply at the top of the circle. Alexi came out. He didn't have much to shoot at and was about to fire away anyway when at the last moment he saw Pudge skating furiously to the far post. Charlie sent a saucer pass over the defenceman's stick to a spot three feet from the post.

"Too far," he cursed himself.

But he'd underestimated his friend's determination. Pudge dove headlong at the puck and managed to slice at it with his stick, redirecting it over Alexi's stacked pads, before sliding into the back boards.

Clank.

The puck hit the post and bounced out. Charlie groaned and smashed the ice with his stick.

Pudge didn't give up, however. The puck lay a few feet to Alexi's right. Before the goaltender could cover up Pudge dove from behind the net and swung his stick — and connected!

A massive roar swept across the arena — goal!

Charlie threw himself on top of Pudge. "Most incredible play I've ever seen," he yelled in his ear.

Zachary launched himself on top, the twins arriving next. Somehow Charlie ended up on the bottom of the pile and couldn't move. He also couldn't have cared less. They'd actually taken the lead. He never really imagined that they'd still be in the game in the third period. For the first time he really believed they could beat the Snow Birds.

The referee blew his whistle. "Line it up," he said. "Game's not over."

They reluctantly ended their celebration. Charlie knew the ref was right. Still eight minutes on the clock

— lots of time. The Snow Birds were too good to quit.

He saw Hilton look at them and cup his hands around his mouth. He couldn't hear a word, though. The Rebels fans were going crazy, clapping wildly and chanting the team name. Hilton waved them to the bench. "Play it safe," he said when they got there. "We need to take some time off the clock. Dump it in deep. One man in. Wingers pick up their checks."

Tweet! Tweet! Tweet!

"Line up, Rebels, or it's a delay-of-game penalty," the referee said.

Charlie lined up quickly. Savard tried to draw it back, but Charlie went in hard, knocking his stick aside and pushing him backwards. He was able to kick the puck to Robert. A short pass to Pudge and a step across the red line, and the puck was in deep, just as Hilton instructed.

"One man in," Hilton called from the bench. "Cover your man."

Over the next few minutes Hilton proved what a good coach does for a team. In the Rebels' first game against the Snow Birds, Dale had adjusted their break-out for the second period. The goals followed soon after. This was not the same Rebels team, however. Hilton had drilled them relentlessly. Rather than mechanically sending one man in deep, they varied the pressure, sometimes sending two, or sending in two and then backing one off. The key was shifting rapidly to close down the passing lanes.

The Rebels continually turned the Snow Birds back and, unaccustomed to being behind, the Snow Birds made uncharacteristic mistakes, forcing bad passes or shooting wide. With a minute to go, Zachary deflected a shot into the crowd. The referee pointed to the face-off circle to Martin's left. Dale called a time out. The Rebels crowded around their coach.

"We'd better be ready for some real pressure," Hilton said. "I expect they'll pull their goalie for an extra man, especially with the faceoff in our zone. All efforts go into getting the puck out. Avoid icing if possible. I'd rather have you dump it into the neutral zone than have an icing because you tried to score from your own end."

He turned to Charlie. "Winning the faceoff is critical. Draw it back to Scott if you can. If not, tie Savard up. Pudge, you come off the wing and fire it out." He took a deep breath. "We're close to a major upset. Play smart — play safe. Off the boards and out. Let's do this, boys."

The Rebels headed to their end. Dale was still explaining a play. This time the referee threatened the Snow Birds with a delay-of-game penalty. When they came out for the faceoff, Charlie saw that the net was empty and the extra man was setting up in the slot. He adopted a reverse grip and lined up quickly. Savard had barely come off since Pudge's goal. He didn't want to give him any more time to rest. Savard put his stick down.

The puck dropped and both centremen swept their sticks through the circle to pull it back. But Charlie was a touch faster. The puck dribbled to Scott, and the Rebels fans cheered. The right winger was on him like a cat, however. He lowered the boom, crushing Scott into the boards. Scott hung tough and held the puck in his skates as the winger poked at it furiously. Then Savard charged in to help — Charlie right next to him. No way he was letting him get free. Charlie spotted Zachary guarding the far side, which gave him an idea.

"Scott! Scott! Kick it behind the net," he said.

Scott did just that, and Charlie one-timed it blindly around the boards. Zachary got there in time to trap the puck with his body. Unfortunately, the defenceman pinched and Zachary couldn't get the puck out. Charlie and Savard raced over. As before, the Snow Birds dug at the puck, while the Rebels made sure it stayed against the boards, out of harm's way. Finally, Savard managed to slip his stick in between Zachary's skates and knock the puck to the corner. Charlie was about to give chase until he saw Nick would get it.

Burnett was cheating into the slot. The left winger and the extra attacker were in front of the net. Zachary and the defenceman, exhausted by their fight for the puck, were still against the boards. That gave Charlie another idea — this time a crazy one. Hilton had told them to play it safe, but instinct took over. A goal would put it away. Instead of staying with Savard, he took off up ice, skating backwards into the gap left by Burnett and his defence partner.

"Nick, up the middle!" he screamed.

Nick barely looked up. He whirled around and fired a blistering pass up the middle. Charlie knew passing up the middle from deep in your own end is dangerous at the best of times; to do it with a one-goal lead, in the semifinals, with thirty seconds left, was verging on suicidal.

But it worked! Over-committed in the slot, Burnett

dove for the puck. Snow Birds fans groaned and Rebels fans cheered as the puck squirted past the star defence-man, and onto Charlie's stick. He carried the puck right to the goal line — for some reason he was convinced he'd miss if he shot — and, from a foot away, he slammed the puck into the netting.

He circled the goal and leaned against the boards. He wanted to enjoy the moment. His teammates were tearing down the ice. Pudge had his stick high over his head. Zachary was gliding on one foot, an arm raised in triumph. Scott banged the ice with his stick, Nick right behind pumping his fist. Charlie couldn't believe it. They'd beaten the Snow Birds, and were into the finals.

His teammates mobbed him.

"*Re-bels! Re-bels! Re-bels!*" they chanted over and over.

27

WILD STYLE

Charlie and Jake stood at centre waiting for the referee and the timekeeper to fix the clock. Charlie shifted his weight from foot to foot. It was taking forever for the game to start, and hanging out with Jake wasn't doing much to settle his nerves.

Jake broke the silence. "How's your head? I felt really bad when you got hurt," he said sarcastically.

"How was the suspension?"

"No big deal. It was worth punching your lights out."

Charlie turned his back on him and drifted towards his own end. The entire season had come down to this one game. They'd played to a 2–2 draw in the first game of the finals. The winner would be the league champions: it was sudden death. Charlie wanted to win more than anything. To do that, he knew he'd have to keep a level head. He turned around.

"Do you ever get tired of being like that — even for a second?"

"You won't last the game, Joyce. That's a promise."

The referee's whistle interrupted.

"Clock's ready. Line 'em up, boys," he said.

Charlie turned to face his own goal for a moment to calm himself. At least he'd shown Jake that he wasn't going to back down. Charlie lined up. The referee waved at both goalies and then dropped the puck. The game was on! Charlie won the draw, and pulled the puck back to Scott.

"Too slow, Jake," he said.

Jake growled and pressed forward. Scott drifted wide to his left, and bounced the puck off the boards. Pudge trapped it, kicked it up to his stick, and fired it deep into the right corner.

Charlie was after it like a jackrabbit. The defenceman barely touched it before Charlie flattened him into the boards. The glass rattled with the impact, and he crumpled to the ice. Charlie dug the puck out of the corner.

The referee whistled the play down and pointed at Charlie, and then pressed his fist into his palm and skated over to the penalty box — a penalty for boarding!

"It's a contact sport," he heard a spectator yell. "Call it fair."

"If you're just gonna let the Wildcats win, then why bother playing?"

The Rebels fans were really giving it to the referee. Charlie wished they would stop. A hostile referee wouldn't help. But the catcalls and jeering continued.

Charlie was too agitated to sit. "Pudge, watch Jake in the slot," he yelled. "Don't give him any time. Scott, just fire it out — nothing fancy. You too, Nick — nothing fancy."

He forced himself to be quiet. Yelling instructions from the penalty box wasn't going to help — they couldn't hear him with all the noise, anyway. The face-off was outside the Wildcats' zone. Jake won the draw against Zachary. The right defenceman hesitated, and then passed it to Roscoe. The powerful right winger skated hard at Scott. Jake was roaring up the middle. Scott had to back up, and Roscoe gained the blue line.

Pudge came over to force him. Scott and Nick settled down low, and Zachary drifted into the slot.

"Good positioning," Charlie said. Then his heart sank. He had forgotten about Liam. Both defencemen were preoccupied with Jake. That left a clear passing lane through the centre of the box to Liam at the inside hash marks.

Charlie jumped to his feet — then sat back down. Nothing he could do. He didn't bother watching. He knew how it would turn out. The roar of the crowd told him that the Wildcats had scored. He opened the door and skated slowly to his bench. Liam had his stick in the air. He and Roscoe punched gloves. Jake was skating back to centre, both arms overhead, nodding to the crowd. Charlie gave the boards a kick as he sat down. Totally his fault — a stupid penalty. Now it was 1–0, with barely thirty seconds off the clock.

"Sorry, guys," he said to no one in particular.

"Bogus call," Zachary said. "We'll get it back."

Hilton put his hand on his shoulder. "Put it behind you," he said softly. "That's their gift. Be patient and we'll get our chances."

Charlie had to wait until five minutes into the second period. Matt attempted to split the defence, and as one defender rode him off to the boards, his stick got tangled up in Matt's skates.

"Tripping," the ref said, sweeping his right hand across his knee.

Hilton leaned over Charlie's shoulder. "That call was almost as bad as the one they called on you," he said. "Perhaps we should take advantage of his generosity. Let's change it up."

Now it was the Wildcats fans' turn to heap abuse on the referee.

"The guy tripped over the blue line."

"Total even-up call. He barely touched him."

"You want my glasses, ref? You need 'em more than me."

Charlie was pumped. This was just what the Rebels needed.

"I'm going to fire it in deep," he told Pudge and Zachary as they skated to the faceoff to the right of the Wildcats' goal. "Let's pressure their D right off the bat."

Jake and Liam came out for the penalty-kill. He'd expected a few insults from Jake, but this time he was all business. Charlie didn't try to win the draw, preferring to push the puck between Jake's legs and into the corner. The Wildcats defenceman got there first.

He must have wished he hadn't, because Pudge was on him and laid a massive hit. The puck squirted free, and Zachary scooped it up, skating to the corner. The Wildcats set up their box. Charlie was at the hash marks near the boards and Zachary slid it to him.

He nodded to Zachary. Perfect set-up for their favourite power-play move — the give-and-go. He passed it down low to Zachary. Charlie skated hard into the seam between the forward and the defenceman and took the return pass. Pudge anticipated the play and occupied the other defenceman in front. Charlie continued across the slot. The goalie flopped to the ice, straining to see him through the legs of the players in front.

He held onto the puck, using Pudge as a screen. The goalie fell to his side, stacking his pads. The top half of the net was wide open. Charlie let the puck fly ten feet from the top of the crease.

He raised his stick, only to see the puck nick the goalie's left arm and flutter end over end over the crossbar, landing on top of the netting. The goalie was still on his back. Charlie put his stick under the netting and flipped the puck back in front.

The crowd was screaming, and a mad scramble ensued. Charlie got two more shots, one that hit the goalie's mask, and another that grazed the outside of the post. The puck went behind the net. Zachary was on it quickly, and feathered a pass to Nick, who was breaking into the slot from the point, his stick held high over his head for a slapshot.

Charlie drove to the net from the left side, slamming into a Wildcats defenceman, which opened up that side for Nick.

"Fire it, Nick," Charlie said.

The goalie was down again, totally screened. A sure goal, Charlie thought. Again, he was wrong. At the last second, the puck hit a rut and skipped over Nick's stick as he was about to shoot.

Jake was first to the puck and he took off like a jackrabbit. Scott was the last man back, but he was no match for Jake in terms of foot speed. Jake pulled away at the red line. Martin crouched deeply and drifted out.

Charlie was the fastest man on the ice, and he flew past the others. But Jake had too much of a head start. Charlie watched as his nemesis faked a forehand, waited for Martin to commit to a butterfly, and then backhanded it up over his shoulder under the crossbar.

If Charlie didn't detest Jake he would have admired the goal. As it was, he felt sick to his stomach. Down two goals already!

Jake jumped up and down, his arms raised in triumph. He looked at Charlie, his mouth curled into a mocking smile.

"Smokin', baby. This is too easy," he said.

Liam threw an arm around Jake's neck.

"Wildcats' championship — love the sound of that."

"Loser Rebels," Jake said. "That sounds better."

"Three periods in hockey," Charlie said. "Clock says we keep playing."

"You must like punishment, Joyce, 'cause this'll only get worse," Jake said.

His teammates arrived to celebrate. Charlie had no desire to continue the trash talk. His heart wasn't really in it. He was too worried about the score. He headed to the bench, where Hilton was already rallying the troops.

"If they play wide open, we keep to our usual game and trade chances. My guess is that won't be the case, and they'll play defensively from here on in. That's not their style, so we may get some breaks if we get pressure in their end. Two goals is nothing, so don't get down on yourselves. You've battled through worse. Be patient, and the goals will come."

Hilton's words proved prophetic. The Wildcats'

offensive-minded play of the first period gave way to a stifling defensive shell. Schultz had ordered his players to protect the lead. Led by Charlie's relentless attacks, the Rebels slowly took over the game, but they couldn't convert on their chances, and the second period ended without a goal.

Charlie and Pudge were leaning against the boards while the goalies switched ends for the start of the third.

"I didn't think the Wildcats could play this type of game," Pudge said.

"They'll make a mistake sometime. All we need is one break," Charlie said.

Matt came over. "This is painful. We gotta get one back. Then things'll loosen up."

"They're lining five guys across their blue line," Scott said. "We gotta dump it in. We can't carry it through that many defenders.

"But keep it away from their goalie," Zachary said. "He's fairly good with the puck.

"Lots of shots," Dylan said from the bench. "We're trying to make the perfect play. Shoot from anywhere."

"Dylan's right," Charlie said. "I'm the worst culprit. We have to shoot — this goalie's no superstar."

"We're making him look good," Nick said.

"Two dumb plays and it's 2–0," Charlie said. "Things have to start going our way."

He just prayed that wasn't wishful thinking.

28

PENALTY BOX

Charlie's prayer seemed destined to go unanswered. The Wildcats had completely shut down the Rebels' offence. They dumped the puck out of their zone at every opportunity, picked up their checks, took the body, and made smart passes. With the puck at his own blue line, he snuck a peek at the clock — eight minutes left. As usual, five Wildcats waited for him to make a move. Zachary and Pudge hovered near the Wildcats' blue line, looking for a long pass. But it was impossible to carry it through, and equally tough to pass. Without much choice, Charlie decided to get over centre and fire it in — for what seemed the hundredth time.

He cut sharply across the Rebels' blue line towards the left boards to avoid one forechecker. Another Wildcat moved forward to stop him. He didn't have much room to manoeuvre, and he still wasn't over the red line. The last thing he wanted was an icing. He faked an inside move, flicked the puck off the boards, and tried to bull his way past. The player wasn't fooled and he pushed him off the puck and into the boards. More out of frustration than anything, Charlie reached out with his right hand, grabbed the player's shoulder, and pulled him backwards. The player fell to the ice. The Wildcats fans immediately cheered in expectation of a penalty.

The puck lay against the boards. Charlie scooped it up half-heartedly. Stupid penalty, he berated himself — obvious holding. Players on both teams, expecting the referee to whistle the play down, stopped skating. Charlie carried it slowly up the boards, until suddenly it dawned on him that the whistle wasn't going to come — the refs weren't calling it. Before the Wildcats could react, Charlie took off and blew past the right defence-man. The left defenceman raced over to head him off. Charlie cut in at the hash marks and braced himself.

Bang!

The two players collided ten feet from the net and crashed to the ice, their momentum carrying them headlong into the goalie, who was knocked clear off his feet. All three players ended up in the net. Charlie struggled to free himself. He saw the referee behind the net, with one hand raised and the other pointing right at him.

He lowered his head. Must be a penalty for goaltender interference — that would kill their chances. Then he saw something black and round nestled in the far corner of the net — the puck!

He pointed feverishly at it. "Ref, it's in — the puck's in. Right there!"

Charlie felt an arm across his chest. A Wildcats player dragged him roughly out of the net and dumped him unceremoniously to the side.

"He ran the goalie," he said. "No goal."

The referee continued to point at the puck.

"Your own player forced him into your goalie. It's a goal."

The referee skated towards the scorekeeper, and moments later the scorekeeper announced to the crowd, "Goal scored by number 8, Charlie Joyce; assist number 3, Scott Slatsky."

The Wildcats fans lost it. A few began banging on the glass with their hands, screeching insults at the top of their lungs.

"Have you lost your mind?"

"Get a life, ref!"

On the ice, the Wildcats players surrounded the beleaguered referee. The goalie was front and centre. He was absolutely livid.

"He ran me down," he said, whacking his pads with his stick. "Are you freakin' kidding me? What game are you watching?"

"Your own man sent him into you," the referee said.

"But I had the puck. He can't knock me into my own net. Where's your bloody whistle? Saving it for Christmas?"

Jake pushed in front of the goalie. He'd come off the bench to argue. "Total goaltender interference," he said.

"Discussion's over. Line up."

"That was the worst call ever. Did you drop your glasses? Joyce throws a guy to the ice, and then runs the goalie. He deserved two penalties, and you're too stupid to even call one."

The referee was skating backwards, Jake following, trailed by his teammates. Schultz stood up on the bench, one foot on the boards.

"Get over here!" he said to the referee. "No way

I'm putting up with that." The referee glared at the coach. "How'd you miss that penalty on number 8? Were you sleepin' or what?"

"You all need to calm down," the ref said, "or you'll be the ones getting a penalty."

"Oh, that makes sense," Jake said. "What planet are you from, Mars or Jupiter?"

"You'd better watch it."

"You're a joke — a bad joke."

The referee held up two fingers and skated to the penalty box.

"Penalty to number 9, Jake Wilkenson," the scorekeeper announced. "Two minutes for unsportsmanlike conduct."

Boom.

Jake smashed his stick against the boards. The sound reverberated around the rink. "You're the most bogus ref ever. You're such a loser you make losers feel cool."

Charlie, who had been watching the drama unfold from centre, saw the ref's face go white. Then the ref slowly touched his hands to his hips.

"Gotta be a misconduct," he said to Pudge.

Jake looked over at Schultz. His coach threw his hands over his head and stepped down from the boards. Jake whacked the boards with his stick again and went into the penalty box, slamming the door so hard it bounced open. Charlie returned to his bench in time to hear the referee explain the call to Hilton.

"He's got a ten-minute misconduct," the referee said, "plus a two-minute penalty. He can come back if the game goes into overtime."

He pushed off to the Wildcats' bench to speak to Schultz.

"Listen up, gentlemen," Hilton said. "I'm making a slight change. I want Charlie's line out — but Scott, if you don't mind, perhaps Matt can take your place at the left point. That'll give us four forwards and a bit more firepower."

"Go for it, Matt," Scott said, giving him a high-five.

"Their best player is in the penalty box," Hilton continued. "We have to take advantage. Dump and chase. When we get control, I want Charlie behind the net. Get it to him. Then Nick, you charge the net. Charlie, he's your first option. Matt, if he's covered, that's your cue to go next. Pudge, peel off and swing around to cover the point. Zachary, you hunt for a rebound."

The referee blasted his whistle, his arms pinned across his chest.

"Line up, boys," Hilton said. He pointed to the faceoff circle. "One more, and we're back in it."

Liam and Roscoe were out to kill Jake's penalty.

"Garbage goal," Liam said, lining up to take the draw. "Here's where we take over."

Charlie knew Liam had a temper. He wondered if he could keep it in check.

"Your goalie makes a nice pillow," Charlie said.

"So will your head."

"Did Jake give you permission to say that?"

"Funny, Joyce."

Anticipating the drop, Charlie swept Liam's stick aside.

"Wait for the puck," the referee said.

Charlie did it again.

"You're out of the circle," the referee shouted.

Thwack.

Liam slashed Charlie on the hip.

"Get a life, Joyce," he said.

The referee grabbed Liam by the arm and fairly catapulted him towards the penalty box.

"What about him?" Liam said.

The referee chopped his right arm with his left hand indicating a slashing penalty.

"Are you some kind of idiot?" Liam screamed.

The referee touched his hips with his hands.

"Two minutes for slashing and a misconduct," the scorekeeper announced.

Stay cool, Joyce, Charlie told himself, and the Rebels have got this game.

Liam screamed at the referee from the boards. The Wildcats parents heaped even more abuse. Schultz was apoplectic.

Hilton waved Charlie over.

"Same strategy as before," he said. "Dump it in. Get control behind the net. First look is Nick, and then to Matt in the slot."

Charlie nodded and skated to his blue line. "Come here, guys," he said. His teammates huddled around him. "We've got a five-on-three for two minutes. This is our chance to tie it up. I get it behind the net, and the two defencemen charge the net. I'll hit whoever's open."

Roscoe took the faceoff, but was content to let Charlie win. The puck came back to Nick. Roscoe hovered at centre. Nick snapped a pass to Zachary on the open wing. He wasted no time firing it into the

Wildcats' zone. The puck flew around the boards to a waiting Pudge, who stopped it at the hash marks. The Wildcats immediately formed their triangle.

Charlie set up behind the net as Hilton instructed. The Rebels passed the puck around to tire the defence a bit, and then Pudge passed it to him along the wall. He trapped the puck with his skate and bounced it onto his stick. Right on cue, Zachary stormed the net and Nick pinched into the slot to the left of the hash marks. Nick was open momentarily, but Roscoe stretched his stick across to take away the passing lane. That left the left side of the ice wide open. Matt timed his rush perfectly. Charlie swung to the right, and flipped Matt a backhand pass. He let a blistering one-timer go from fifteen feet. Charlie had a perfect view as the puck sailed over the goalie's glove and into the top corner.

"Scores!"

The Rebels fans rose as one and cheered. Charlie threw his arms around Matt.

"How sweet is this!" Matt said.

"Goal of the century," Charlie said.

"Gentlemen, start your engines," Zachary said, banging their helmets with his glove.

"We've still got a one-man advantage," Pudge said. "We can break this tie."

"They're falling apart," Charlie said. "Let's line up fast and get right to work."

Jake's minor penalty was over because they'd scored. Liam still had a minute and a half to go in his, so the Rebels would enjoy a lengthy five-on-four. Roscoe took the draw again. He wasn't a natural centre, however. Charlie took advantage of his lack of experience. Rather than draw the puck back, he pushed it towards the Wildcats' end and continued forward in one motion. Roscoe was still hunched over for the face-off, stick on the ice, while Charlie was motoring in on the defence. He slid the puck to Zachary. The right winger bore down on the left defenceman. Zachary gained the zone and cut hard to his left, where he dropped the puck for Charlie. He then charged sharply up ice towards the net.

Charlie picked up the puck in full flight. At the top of the circle, he raised his stick high above his head for a slapshot. The left defenceman dropped to his knees — prematurely. Charlie faked the shot, leaving the Wildcats defender flailing his stick at him as he swept by. The right defenceman had Zachary covered by the post. But when Charlie closed in on the net, he left Zachary and dropped to block the shot. Charlie promptly fired a hard pass to Zachary. The goalie had also overplayed Charlie. The net was wide open. Zachary had time to stop the puck and carefully fire it in.

"Only up by one," Charlie said, after he and his teammates congratulated each other. "We need the insurance goal. Keep up the pressure."

That came a minute later when Jonathon snuck one in on a wraparound to the goalie's stick side. Charlie leaned over the boards and smacked Jonathon's glove as he came by to celebrate. Charlie felt happy for him. This was only his fifth goal all year.

"Awesome play," he said.

"Let's keep this party going," Jonathon said.

"One more goal, and this baby's ours," Charlie said, shifting on for Matt.

Only a little over five minutes remained, and they had a two-goal lead, but he was still nervous. The Wildcats would be right back in it if they scored. He lined up for the faceoff. A water bottle skidded past him. He straightened up.

"Where did that come from?" he said to no one in particular.

Another water bottle skipped across the ice, and then a stick. Schultz was standing on the boards holding several sticks over his head. "Worst reffing I've seen in thirty years of coaching!" His face was purple with rage.

Charlie had never seen an adult that angry.

"You're worse than blind — you're dumb too. Read the rule book one day, or do hockey a favour and quit refereeing."

Charlie felt sorry for the referee. Maybe he'd missed a call or two. But this wasn't the NHL. The referee skated to the Wildcats' bench.

"Get your players to pick up those water bottles and the stick. You just got yourself a bench minor. Disrupt the game again and you'll have to leave."

Schultz threw the sticks he was still holding and the referee had to jump out of the way.

"I'm more than happy to leave," he said. "In fact, we'll all leave. This game is totally fixed. Come on, boys. We don't need this. Into the dressing room — now."

The Wildcats players were bewildered. No one moved, uncertain as to what was happening.

"Are you listening? I said into the dressing room!" Schultz repeated. "Move it."

The players filed out the door and headed across the

rink to the door leading to the dressing rooms. Charlie was almost as bewildered as the Wildcats. They'd been winning only a few minutes ago — and now they were quitting!

"It's like they're little kids," he said to Pudge.

"That's Schultz for you," Pudge said. "He's Mr. Happy when he's winning — and a total jerk when he loses."

"Kind of takes the fun out of things," Zachary said. "I mean . . . what happens now? There's still 5:20 on the clock."

The scorekeeper answered the question.

"The Wildcats have forfeited," he announced. "The Rebels have won the championship. Final score is Rebels 4–Wildcats 2."

The crowd remained quiet. Everyone was in a state of shock.

"This feels weird," Charlie said. "Never won a championship without finishing the game."

"It's like they cheated us out of our win," Pudge said.

"I'd feel kind of lame charging Martin," Zachary said.

He was still in his net, arms draped over the cross-bar.

"Forget that," Charlie said. "After this season, we deserve to celebrate." He turned to his teammates. "Don't know about you guys, but here's one guy who will take this win. Wildcats want to quit? That's their problem."

He threw his gloves into the air and raced to Martin, jumping up and down.

"You're a champion, dude!" he said to the goalie.

He spun him around in a bear hug. The next second, he and Martin were lying on the ice. Pudge and Zachary had bowled them over.

"Who're the champs?" Charlie shouted.

"The Rebels!" his teammates chorused.

Scott and Nick piled on next, and soon all the players formed a massive jumble of arms and legs. They got up and continued congratulating each other. Matt was too excited to speak. He traded head butts with each teammate. Zachary leaned against the crossbar and yelled, "Rebels is the champs — dig it."

Even Hilton joined the fun. He went around to each player, shaking hands and patting helmets. "You should be proud of yourself," he said to Charlie. "You answered Jake in spades — by outplaying him when it counted. Pressure games bring out the best in people — or the worst. It brought out the best in you."

"Thanks, Coach," he said. "And thanks for doing this — the coaching, I mean. Couldn't have done it without you. When I think about what the team was like back in December . . ."

Hilton laughed loudly, which was not something Charlie heard him do often. He looked genuinely happy.

"Ladies and gentlemen," blared a voice from the loudspeakers. "Can we have your attention at centre ice for the medal ceremony."

Steve Roberts and his mother waved to the crowd. Next to them stood a long table covered in trophies. Charlie led his teammates to the blue line.

Steve held a microphone.

"I want to congratulate the East Metro Hockey League triple-A minor bantam champs — the Rebels." The crowd cheered and the players banged their sticks on the ice.

"Normally, we'd hand out trophies to the runners-up first . . . but given the circumstances, perhaps we'll get right to it." The crowd laughed. "Rebels, come get your trophies!"

Steve called each player's name and shook his hand, and his mother handed out the trophies. He called Charlie's name last, and gave him his trophy and the championship cup. Charlie held the cup over his head and the Rebels and their fans cheered loudly. Steve took the microphone again.

"We have one more trophy to award, for Most Valuable Player." He picked up a trophy. "I put a lot of thought into this one. Some people say an MVP should be the best player in the league, or the guy with the most goals. I think it's for the player who contributes the most to his team. As we all know, the Rebels are an unusual organization. The players ran the team themselves. They didn't even have a coach until halfway through the season. And, as the parents of these boys know very well, they practised at six in the morning!

"One player took the initiative to organize the team. He missed some games due to an injury, but led his team in scoring in the regular season and the playoffs. He stood out all year with his creative and unselfish play. Let's have a rousing cheer for this year's MVP, Charlie Joyce!"

He couldn't believe it! He'd just assumed J.C. Savard, Burnett, or maybe even Jake would win it. His teammates whacked his shoulder pads and pounded his helmet.

"Congrats, Charlie," Steve said. "You guys surprised me. I still remember you coming into my office all those months ago. Never thought you'd make it this far."

"Neither did I," Charlie said.

"I knew you were a good boy," Steve's mom added.

Charlie held the trophy over his head, and the crowd cheered even louder than before. His teammates crowded around him.

"How about a picture?" Brent was on the ice holding a camera. "I need a picture for the store. First time I sponsor a team, and it wins the championship. I like it."

Charlie put the championship cup on the ice and they all flopped down around it. Charlie noticed Hilton off to the side.

"Coach, you gotta get in this picture too," he said.

"Yeah, come on."

"Get in here."

Hilton laughed and joined them.

"You too, Grandpa — and Jeffrey," Charlie said.

"Give me that championship smile," Brent said.

Charlie didn't need to be asked.

KEEPIN' IT GOING

Charlie sat on the front steps of his house. He flipped a Frisbee to Pudge.

"It's amazing," Charlie said. "The music's blaring downstairs — and I can still hear Scott."

"What's he calling himself now?"

"Righteous King of Hip Hop."

Charlie had invited his teammates to his house after the game. News spread, though, and a bunch of the kids from school who'd watched the game were also there. They'd been dancing downstairs for the past half an hour.

The trophies were arranged on the front steps. Scott had seen to that. "To make sure people understand there's a new champ in town," he'd said.

Pudge picked up a trophy. "The only thing wrong with the game was the Wildcats didn't have to watch us get our hardware," he said.

"I'm not gonna forget that game any time soon," Charlie said. "It was totally random. I wonder what the league will do with Schultz. I still can't believe he freaked out in the championship game."

"No shortage of memories from this season," Pudge said.

"Remember me and you sitting alone in that ice box of a dressing room before practice?" Charlie said.

"Or seeing those pink sweaters for the first time."

"What about the car wash?" Charlie said.

"That was definitely a low point."

"My low point was Dunn kicking me off the team. Too weird to think how it turned out."

"Speaking of low points, aren't you forgetting the concussion?"

"I'd like to forget about Jake." He stared at the ground for a second before looking Pudge in the eye. "What I won't forget is a guy I know who told me to put the concussion and the fight behind me and just play hockey."

Pudge kicked at the steps a few times. He laughed and picked up the Frisbee lying to the side. "Wanna toss the bean around a bit more before going back downstairs?"

Charlie nodded emphatically. After a few throws, Charlie let loose a high one that grazed Pudge's fingertips and sailed over the road onto the lawn across the street.

"I get it! I get it!"

Josh and his father were crossing the street. Josh picked up the Frisbee.

"Hi, Chawie. Hi, Fudge."

"Hi, Josh."

"That was quite a game," Josh's dad said.

"Didn't know you were there," Charlie said.

"Dunn kept telling everyone at work how you guys were going to flame out. Can't tell you how great it felt to see you pull it off — and believe me, this will be like a dagger in Dunn's heart. It'll kill him."

"It was fun," Pudge said.

"Can I hold that? I like it," Josh said, pointing to the MVP trophy. "What is it?"

"That's Charlie's trophy," his dad said.

"I want it," Josh said.

"Now, Josh. Charlie worked hard for that. It's his."

Charlie took it from the steps.

"I'd like you to have it, Josh. Will you take good care of it for me?"

Josh's grin seemed too big for his face. He threw the Frisbee aside and hugged the trophy to his little chest.

"My twophy!"

They all laughed.

"Are you sure?" Josh's dad asked.

Charlie nodded and pointed to the other trophies. "These are more important."

"Thanks, Charlie. When he loses interest I'll see that it returns to its rightful owner. As for this fellow," he picked his son up, "it's time to get ready for bed. Say goodnight, Josh."

"Goodnight, Chawie. Goodnight, Fudge," Josh said, as his father carried him home.

The door opened and Scott, Nick, Matt and Zachary stormed out.

"I didn't think you guys would ever leave the dance floor," Charlie said.

"We were getting nervous — you two all alone with our babies," Scott said. He took a trophy and cradled it in his arms.

"Now that you mention it, I was thinking these

would look good in my room," Charlie said. "They like me."

Pudge elbowed Charlie.

"There's Hilton and Brent," he said.

The two men got out of a van and came over.

"How's it going, gentlemen?" Hilton said.

"No complaints," Charlie said. "How about you?"

"None that I can think of," Hilton replied. "Brent and I found ourselves talking about the season after the game, and before we knew it we'd been sitting in the stands for an hour. I figured you'd all still be here, and we decided to drop by.

"I hope two old men won't dampen the party," Brent said.

"Not at all," Charlie said. "Wouldn't be right if you missed it."

"We got to talking about the team's future," Hilton said. "I confess I had a great time coaching. There's something special about this group. You have a chemistry that's hard to find. I liked being part of it — and clearly, the result was satisfactory."

"I don't know about that," Scott said. "I kinda thought the MVP should've come my way. You may not know this, but most of the guys called me The Inspiration."

"Don't you mean The Perspiration?" Nick said.

Scott pretended to be shocked. "So that's why everyone keeps giving me underarm deodorant."

"That's part of it," Nick said.

"You were saying, Coach?" Charlie said. He had a feeling Hilton had something important to say.

"I was thinking — if you are all agreeable, that is —

that I'd like to keep this team together for next year. And I'd definitely like to stay on as your coach."

"That sounds like a plan to me," Charlie said. "What do you guys think?"

"Depends on the money," Scott said. "I'll have to discuss it with my agent."

"You mean your teddy bear," Nick put in.

"Don't tell them about Teddy," Scott said. He pretended to cry.

"I also want to be a part of this," Brent said. "I got some great publicity from the team. Sales picked up, the word got out about the store, and things are looking up. I'm starting renovations soon, which will give me way more space for new equipment. Next year I'll be able to sponsor you properly. Maybe not like Dunn, but I'll do my best."

"The last thing we want is for you to be anything like Dunn," Charlie said. "This is almost as great as winning the championship. I'm ready to practise right now."

"I can get my equipment and be back in ten minutes," Matt said.

"Mine's in Charlie's garage," Zachary said. "I'll meet you at the rink."

Hilton laughed. "Take the day off. Now tell me, where can I find your mother?"

"She's usually in the kitchen," Charlie said.

"I'll start there. See you in a bit, boys."

He and Brent went inside.

Just then, Edward Shaw showed up. "Did I just see Brent Sanderson and your coach go inside?"

Charlie got up and shook his hand. "Nice to see you, Mr. Shaw," he said.

"I told you, it's Edward," he said good-naturedly. "Your mom asked me to come by after the game. I hope you don't mind."

"Of course not," Charlie said.

"It was nice to see you all do so well today," Edward said.

"We appreciate that," Charlie said. And he meant it. He'd never forget Edward's kindness on the day Dunn kicked him off the Hawks.

"Couldn't miss my team playing in the finals. In fact, I saw most of your home games too. I confess I'm starting to like hockey. I'm already looking forward to next season. Will you be having a team again?"

Charlie grinned. "It looks like we will."

"Marvelous news. I can hardly wait." He patted Charlie on the shoulder. "I should go in and say hello to your mom."

"Try the kitchen," he said.

The Rebels were most definitely on a roll — and it didn't seem that long ago when Charlie didn't even have a team to play on.

30

THE FUNKY CHICKEN

"Dudes, I have been waiting a long time to redeem myself," Zachary announced.

"What did you do wrong?" Charlie said.

"Wait here," he replied, leaping down the steps. He ran to the garage and emerged wearing a helmet and two elbow pads, holding a skateboard.

"I missed landing a jump from the top of these stairs the night you and Pudge told us about the Rebels. Seems only fitting I try again."

"Awesome," Scott said. "We get to see Zachary wipe out again."

"Not likely, dude," Zachary said.

They cleared the trophies from the steps.

"That looks a bit like my board," Charlie said.

"Small price to pay for the glory," Zachary said.

He got on the board, flashed a thumbs-up, and pushed off with his left foot. At the top of the steps he bounced hard on the board, bending down low at the same time. He flew in the air and, at the last second pushed back on the heel. His rear wheels skinned the tip of the bottom stair, but he managed to hold his balance. Charlie thought his rickety old board would snap in half when he landed, but by some miracle it held together, and Zachary raised his arms in triumph.

"Who's your daddy?" he said.

"Who's completely whacked?" Charlie answered.

"Who was crazy enough to let me use his board?" Zachary replied.

Charlie and Zachary traded high-fives.

"One day, Zachary, you're truly gonna kill yourself," Charlie said.

"But not today!" Zachary shot back.

Matt was putting the trophies back on the steps.

"Charlie, where's the MVP trophy? I swear I saw it here," Matt said.

Charlie pointed across the street. By coincidence, Josh had come out the door moments before in his pajamas holding the trophy.

"I found the real MVP and gave it to him."

"I don't remember him playing many games," Matt said.

"You weren't at the street hockey game in my driveway before the season. If Dunn hadn't almost run Josh over, he never would have stopped the car and invited us to the Hawks tryouts. The Rebels would never have been born."

"I guess we all underestimated that little dude," Zachary said.

"He's my new hero," Scott said.

"Goodnight, Chawie!" Josh yelled.

"Goodnight, Josh," they all yelled back.

Josh's mom came outside, waved, and picked Josh up in her arms. He held the trophy over his head as his mom carried him in.

"Time for some Rebels to take over the dance floor," Charlie said.

"You've gained some confidence since your last dance," Pudge said.

"No point being afraid," Charlie said. "I learned that this season."

"Let's do it, guys," Scott said.

They charged up the steps, chanting, "Re-bels! Re-bels!" Charlie lagged behind. He felt like being alone for a minute. Pudge's comment had brought up some painful memories. Now that the season was over he could admit to himself that he'd been downright afraid of Jake. But ultimately he'd faced up to him. And Jake had proven himself a coward by losing his temper and getting those penalties. His dad had told him a thousand times that cowards are selfish, that they always let others down when the game is on the line.

The memory of his dad made him sad, but this time it was in a good way. He liked having those memories — they were the only things he had left.

"Are you coming in?"

Julia had come out onto the porch.

Charlie felt embarrassed being outside by himself. "I was just getting some fresh air. Trying to soak it all in."

"It was a lot of fun . . . watching the games," she said. "You were terrific. I thought the whole team . . . sort of followed you."

She blushed and looked down at the steps. He could tell she was nervous too. Why couldn't he just talk to this girl? He liked her, and yet there always seemed to be something unspoken between them that made talking hard. Time to put an end to that, he decided.

"There's a little thing that's been bugging me for a while," he said. "Something I want to say to you."

The expression on her face turned serious.

"I wanted to apologize for what I did at the dance — or, how I acted. I was messed by the concussion . . ." He bit his lip and shook his head. "Scratch that. I blamed the concussion for every stupid thing I did — and believe me, I did a lot of stupid things. The concussion had nothing to do with any of it. Anyway, at the dance, I was maybe a bit nervous and . . . Jake and his crew were staring at me . . . and I think I sounded sort of dumb when we were talking by the doors before I left."

"Is that why you've been . . . I don't know . . . avoiding me?"

She looked up him. He noticed that her hair was down by her shoulders. Usually she wore it in a ponytail.

He folded his arms and nodded. "I've been a jerk. Don't take it personally. I've been a jerk to my friends also. I didn't mean to avoid you or anyone. To be honest, the fight with Jake, and his bragging about it all over school, I just figured . . ."

"What did you figure?" she asked in a soft voice.

He leaned back against the railing. "I figured that . . . maybe people wouldn't want to hang out with me, not after Jake made me look so lame. That maybe people would prefer to hang with Jake and his friends."

"And why would I want to do that?"

"Well . . . he did knock me around pretty good — and you did dance with him."

She brushed a hair from her face and raised her chin. "I told you — I danced to be polite." She looked him square in the eye. "I came to your games because I wanted to."

Charlie felt himself flush.

"I'm glad you did — come to the games, I mean."

She laughed. "My team choked and lost in the quarterfinals, so I had time to kill."

Charlie thought she looked kind of cute with her hair down and her nose all scrunched up. He laughed too, and felt his nervousness disappear. He thought about how he'd underestimated his friends, assuming they'd drop him because he lost a fight. He understood how lucky he was to have buds like Pudge, Scott, Nick, Zachary, Matt and all the guys on the team. It seemed he'd underestimated Julia too. He was lucky she was giving him a second chance.

He remembered something from their conversation at the school dance.

"I was about to ask you to dance before Pudge said we had to go," he said. "And you did say it's rude to refuse to dance with a guy . . . at least, a guy you know and who asks politely . . ."

Her expression changed to a half-smile.

"So . . . do you want to dance . . . with me?" he asked.

She smiled. "I won't dance with you to be polite. I'll do it because I want to."

Charlie felt himself blush, and Julia lowered her gaze.

"Let's go downstairs," he said, holding the door for her. "Who knows what Scott's up to."

When they walked in, Scott was standing on a chair in the middle of the room.

"The Rebels got the pink sweaters; the Rebels got

the sponsor; the Rebels got the coach . . . and the Rebels got themselves the trophy."

Everyone cheered.

"Now all that's left is the team dance. Any ideas?"

"Hit the music," Charlie said. "The Rebels do the funky chicken!"

The music started, and Charlie and Scott started to flap their arms and hop around the room — and then all the kids copied them. Soon everyone was laughing so hard they could hardly move. When the song changed, Charlie hopped over to Julia, who was laughing hysterically.

"Is this what you call dancing with me?" she said.

"How about two dances?" he said seriously.

"That might break the rule, but I'll make an exception in your case."

They started to dance. A few of his friends caught his eye and winked or gave him a thumbs-up. He knew it was all in fun and he didn't let it bug him. Why should it? Any guy would be proud to dance with Julia.

The song changed, and he and Julia continued to dance together. The good feeling from the win had carried over to the party, and everyone was having a great time. After a few more songs, Scott jumped up on a chair again.

"Turn down the music for a minute, please. I need everyone's attention." He held his hands over his head until they quieted down. "I would like to announce the start of the First Annual Rebels Dance-Till-You-Drop Contest. I will be the judge, obviously." Charlie led everyone in booing. "Okay, I'll allow Alexandra to be the girls' representative." That was greeted by cheers and whistles. "And now for our first contestants . . ." Nick did a drum roll on the wall. "I give you none other than Charlie 'MVP' Joyce and his dance partner, Julia Chow."

A few weeks ago he would have been mortified. Now he found he liked the sound of it.

"We can't let Scott get away with this," Julia whispered in his ear.

"He's goin' down," he whispered back.

Everyone formed a circle around them and clapped to the beat as he and Julia danced. Charlie took Julia by the waist and started twirling her around. They spun faster and faster and then, without warning, they crashed into Scott who was still on the chair. All three tumbled to the floor.

"Did we win?" Charlie asked.

"You're disqualified," Scott replied. "And I have no choice but to give you two a dance misconduct penalty."

Charlie helped Julia up. "So, who can top that?" Charlie said.

Nick winked at them and took Rebecca onto the floor.

"I think everyone's waited long enough to see me dance," he said.

"This could get ugly," Scott said.

Nick shocked Charlie by busting some impressive moves. Apparently, he'd also learned a few things since the school dance.

Julia put her hand on his shoulder and leaned over to him. "I'm not sure we're going to win the dance contest," she giggled.

"I think we did okay," he said.

Besides, he'd won enough for one day. He actually felt sorry for Jake. He would never get the chance to feel like this. He was too busy acting cool. Jake had actually done him a favour when he gave him the concussion. It had knocked some sense into him — although it took a long time for him to understand that. Maybe he didn't deserve to feel this great, but he did! And that was good enough for him.

ABOUT THE AUTHOR

David Skuy spent most of his childhood playing one sport or another — hockey, soccer, football, rugby. Now he is a writer and lawyer who lives in Toronto, Ontario with his wife and two kids. He still plays hockey once a week and remains a die-hard Leafs fan.

He began writing the Game Time series to try to capture the competition, the challenges, the friendships and the rivalries that make sports so much fun.

The Game Time series:

Off the Crossbar
Rebel Power Play